D0881129

That Day in Gordon

That Day in Gordon

A NOVEL BY

Raymond H. Abbott

THE VANGUARD PRESS
NEW YORK

Library of Congress Cataloging-in-Publication Data
Abbott, Raymond.
That day in Gordon.
I. Title.
PS3551.B265T46   1986   813'.54   86-1691
ISBN 0-8149-0924-8

Designer: Tom Bevans
Jacket by: Tony Parillo
Manufactured in the United States of America.

That Day in Gordon

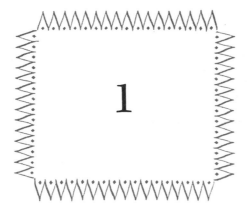

1

WHATEVER IT was was still behind him. Closer, he thought as he turned to get a better look. It was a coyote, he was fairly sure of that, and probably one full grown, although he had never heard of coyotes following a man the way this one did—most were much too timid. But for a half-starved animal any-thing was possible. When he got home to Corn Creek nobody would believe this. They would say it was his imagination or that he was drunk and that a coyote wouldn't follow a man. Even Jim Bennion might look at him funny when he told him.

He was almost certain the snowstorm wasn't

going to become a full-blown blizzard, as they sometimes were when the wind came out of the northwest. But the wind had held steady in the three or four miles he had hiked. He must have gone that far by now.

If that brave coyote out there came closer, he might at least get to see it and be certain it was a coyote and not something else. But what else could it be? Certainly not a wolf. There hadn't been a wolf-sighting in South Dakota in many years, maybe even in his lifetime. Besides, it was too small to be a wolf. He had seen that much of the critter to know this. There was a bushy tail on the small body that he saw when he had turned fast an hour before. He only hoped it wasn't some kind of wild dog. He would much rather be followed by a coyote, even a wolf, than a wild dog. Wild dogs were mighty vicious.

Although ranchers, and especially sheep-herders, thought he was nuts, he kind of liked coyotes, but then, white ranchers considered everything Indians thought or did crazy. But it was the ranchers who were the crazy ones, what with their chasing around after coyotes with poisons, even explosives tied to meat, and airplanes too. All this to kill coyotes, which weren't all that easy to kill. They were plenty smart.

It had been a week since he had been home to

Corn Creek. Everybody in his family was certain to be worried about him. They had heard, he was sure, that he had been released from the Rosebud jail almost a week before.

And his friend Bennion would ask about him too. He could picture Bennion traipsing down back to visit with his family and then all his questions. He wasn't like a lot of white people who gave up easy when trying to get information out of Indians. He'd say, "When did you hear from him last? Is he out of jail? Doris Mae told me he got out of jail four or five days ago, so where is he now?" He would go on in this way until he had all the information he wanted and then would conclude he was off getting himself wild-assed drunk again, and this after having spent two weeks in jail for drunkenness and disorderly conduct.

What Bennion wouldn't guess, however, was that he had been in jail away from the reservation in Nebraska, where the sentences were stiffer, sometimes up to two months for a simple charge of intoxication in a public place. But he had gotten a mere three days and he didn't know why except that the Valentine jail was full of Indians from the reservation. He had it figured that somebody wanted to keep the ones already in the can more than they wanted him, because they released him without even a court appearance. Of course he hadn't put up any kind of fuss when they arrested him, which made a big difference. And some of those Pine Ridge Indians in there were very nasty fellows and very uncooperative when they got arrested. But it was his experience that Pine Ridge Indians weren't just unfriendly toward white people. No sir, they often weren't very friendly toward other Indians. They seemed to harbor a special dislike for members of his tribe, the Brulé band of Sioux at Rosebud, which borders the Pine Ridge Reservation on the east side.

Nobody better call Pine Ridge Indians friendly to his face, not when it was their idea of a joke to push out an Indian brother in a snowstorm, miles from nowhere. That's what they had done to him, and this after he had gone and bought them not one but two six packs. There was no warning, no argument. Nothing. About twenty miles out of Valentine the driver stopped and said, "Get out, you fucker." "Walk home, you asshole," somebody else hollered. At first he thought they must be joking. They weren't.

It was about a half hour out of the car, while walking toward Mission Town and the reservation, that he noticed he was being followed. It was the coyote. Of all the crazy things. Thank God he was warm enough. The coat he wore had a hood and heavy padding in the shoulders and arms and a

4

thick, warm lining. It was one of hundreds of surplus military jackets the tribe had received from the Air Force base at Rapid City. The tribal officials gave a coat to anybody who wanted one, provided he didn't have a job or steady income, which this year covered about everybody on the reservation. There were few jobs to be found after recent federal cutbacks. So he got his good warm coat when he left the Rosebud jail and was damn glad he had it, for when he was arrested the first time he had had a light green cloth coat. By this time he would have frozen to death in that coat.

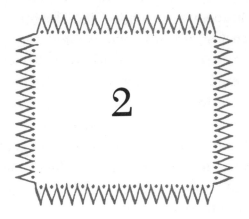

2

IT WAS AFTER two A.M. when he had left Valentine,
so he had to have been walking now for two hours.
It must be four A.M. at least, he thought. Dawn
couldn't be very far away.

The wind was less strong now, which told him
almost for sure that the storm was not a real blizzard. A man could stand about an hour of the wind
and cold with a prairie blizzard and no matter how
warm his coat. After that he would freeze to death.

Still behind him was that damn coyote. A determined critter, he was. He hadn't caught sight of
him for at least an hour, but he felt his presence out

there. At first he had feared him. Now he didn't. If circumstances were different he might have welcomed the company of a coyote on a lonely walk on a snowy night. At best, the coyote's presence was disconcerting. He was puzzled. Why would a coyote be so determined? Poor animal. It had been such a hard winter for man and beast. It wasn't so much that there had been that much snow—there hadn't—but the cold was unrelenting. In his thirty-five years he hadn't known anything like it. His father sometimes talked about other hard winters, but those winters were remembered for the heavy snowfall, not the severe cold. This cold had begun in November. Below zero and colder for weeks now, and a shortage of firewood on the reservation. It was late in March.

He tried to put the coyote out of his mind. He hiked in the direction he knew was the reservation and Mission Town. There were only two ways to go—straight ahead or back from where he came, and that would mean Valentine and he didn't wish to go there again, nor was he welcome there.

When it began to get light he was confident his coyote friend would leave him, and quick.

"I will outwalk you, you cunning critter," he said, grinning for the first time since he had been put out of the car. He felt stronger. That coyote must be hoping I will fall down from exhaustion and die of the cold and then he might get to eat my remains. Coyotes weren't known to do that kind of thing to a man, but with the combination of snow and cold, anything might be possible.

There ought to be traffic soon, he thought. A state plow truck maybe. They came through once a day at least. The snow was drifting across the highway so traffic could barely pass. What traffic? There was none at four A.M. on a snowy night on a rural Nebraska highway.

His confidence was shaken when he recognized a hill with a water windmill on it that he knew to be located at least ten miles out of Mission Town. That meant he was much farther out of town than he had estimated. Could he walk another ten miles?

There were no lights on the car as it came up behind him, and considering the road conditions, it was traveling much too fast. And before it got to where he could hear the roar of the engine above the wind, the car fishtailed after striking a snowdrift and the back fender struck him hard, tossing him into a snowdrift a few feet off the highway. He figured the car must be filled with more drunken Indians. He saw it straighten out and resume its course toward Mission Town. In a moment all he could see was one dim red taillight. Then he saw nothing as he passed out. The occupants of the car hadn't seen him. And he had guessed right that the car held Indians returning from an evening of partying in the Nebraska bars.

The coyote was still out there, as he had known it was. It moved closer now, sensing something had happened to the man. With great caution and fear, it came closer. Its instincts said. "Don't go near the smell of a man." It was a full-grown coyote, but small and ragged, with its winter coat torn and thin—perhaps from injuries in fights, fights with other animals for what little food there was that winter. The animal looked like it was starving.

It stopped on the edge of the road where the car had skidded and hit the Indian. It looked around as if to see if there were other signs of men around. Then, very slowly and with caution, it moved toward the body that lay in the snow. Twice the coyote stopped and sniffed the wind and then moved closer. When it reached the Indian, it sniffed him, knowing there was still warmth and life in the man, yet somehow understanding he was injured and no threat. When the man moved and let out a low moan, the coyote jumped away but did not leave. Then it moved closer once more and gently nudged him, as if challenging him to make another sound or move again or even get up and start walking.

But he could not move. He was semiconscious and thought the coyote was standing near him, perhaps over him, as if to say it is time to get up and get moving.

How long the coyote stood there he did not know, although later there were all sorts of estimates. The incident became a topic of much discussion on the reservation. But stand there the coyote did, perhaps for as long as a half hour, until the expected snowplow appeared and the driver saw the coyote watching over something lying in the snow. He stopped to investigate and the coyote fled. It was then that the driver saw the object was the body of a man. He quickly radioed the Mission Town sheriff for help, and later he said he might have gone right on by the Indian had the coyote not been standing there like a sentry.

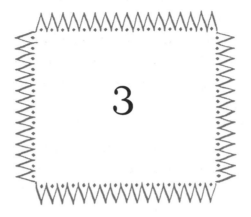

3

ONE OF THE Mission Town police officers was a tall white man with a stomach that hung over his belt. He wore jeans and a cowboy hat. He was half-time rancher and half-time deputy officer. His partner was a much smaller man who was about one-tenth Indian, which in the eyes of the white man made him an Indian just the same. They picked up Black Horse from the snow and carried him to the car.

"This fucking idiot is as drunk as a skunk," the larger man said. "Smell the booze on him."

The other man didn't reply. He nodded his head that he had heard and agreed with what was said.

The first man went on. He was used to his quiet partner.

"Goddamn Indians don't even know 'nough to come in out of the snow. I suppose it would be one less drunk to pick up if we didn't find him. Who is this guy, you know him?"

Again the other man didn't answer. He shook his head. He didn't know the injured man, but he thought he might have remembered having him in the jail once or twice before. He was not one of their regulars, though.

The two men were rough in the way they carried the injured man to the police car. They hadn't meant to hurt him or to be especially rough, but walking in deep snow and carrying a man passed out wasn't that easy. They dropped him in the back seat of the car. Pain shot up his back as he momentarily came around and heard the voices of the two police officers. Then everything was black again. He remembered nothing more until he woke up in the Mission Town jail.

Mission Town is little more than a spot on the map where two highways cross the flat prairie. It is located in the heart of the Rosebud Sioux Indian Reservation in south-central South Dakota. The town consists of two or three gas stations, two motels, two bars (there had been three, but Irish's Bar had rather mysteriously burned down a few

12

months before). There was also a bank, a feed store, a general store called Art's, a dairy whip, and recently a bowling lane with a restaurant connected. Mission was a typical plains town in South Dakota or Nebraska except that it was located smack in the middle of an Indian reservation, which made it a very different kind of town. Even though the town was incorporated with its own charter and elected officers, including a mayor, more than half its citizenry were Sioux Indians. But the town didn't come under the jurisdiction of the tribal government, except for a subdivision called Antelope on the edge of Mission, which was on tribal land.

The town jail had a sign on the outside that read, "Heartbreak Hotel." It was located in the center of Mission across the street from Art's General Store. The jail was small and would hold no more than six or seven prisoners, and then only in the most crowded conditions. It had a reputation for being a tough jail, with reports of Indians being chained to the walls and sometimes severely beaten. But those incidents were now mostly a thing of the past, because pressure to clean up the jail had been considerable. Pressure came mostly from the tribe and the federal government. And since a lot of federal money went into Mission because of the large Indian community there and on the reservation that surrounded it on all sides, the federal influence was significant. Mission could not easily afford to turn its back on the federal money. Most all of its community services and construction projects were paid for with money from Washington.

The white chief of police was appointed by the mayor with the approval of the city council. He was known to remark that dealing with belligerent Indians required a toughness on his part and that of his deputies. He said the bars in Mission were just about always full of drunk Indians who frequently were in a fighting mood.

"I have to come down hard on some of those suckers or they would run over me," he said often at council meetings. His quotes frequently appeared in the town's weekly newspaper, the *Todd County Gazette.*

He would also brag how many of his Indian prisoners came back to see him when they were sober to thank him for his firmness. Thank him, so the story was told, for not permitting fighting and killing and destruction of property to go unpunished in Mission as it did in so many off-reservation towns, places like White Clay near the Pine Ridge Reservation. White Clay was by reputation the toughest town in the territory.

When Black Horse woke up in the Mission

Town jail he wasn't sure where he was. Then he guessed what had happened. He was found along the highway, thought to be passed-out drunk but not seriously injured, and was therefore hauled into the Mission Town lockup. It was standard procedure in and around an Indian reservation. Everybody knew this.

When he tried to move, the pain again shot up his back, and when he placed a little weight on his right leg there was still more pain. He was sure the leg was broken. He called out for the chief. He knew the man a little.

"Hey, somebody. I think my leg is busted. You hear me out there, Chief?"

There was no answer. Then he heard a chair move, and footsteps.

An officer appeared. It was the same large white man who had picked him out of the snowdrift. He didn't know this, however.

"Well, you're sober now, are you? I suppose you want out. That it, mister? What's your name? We've got to have a name—I don't know why. Sometimes you guys come and go so fast."

"Elijah, Elijah Black Horse," he said in a soft voice, trying to ignore the man's comments. The pain in his back was worse. The police always thought the same thing when it came to Indians and drinking.

15

"Where is the chief? I want to see him."

"Just hold a mite, mister. I don't know where he is at all the time. I ain't his keeper. He might be off someplace picking another drunk out of the ditch. Your people keep us mighty busy. Mighty busy, yes sir.

The man smiled. He was enjoying this talk because he could see that the Indian wasn't.

"I said I think my leg's busted, Deputy," Black Horse said again. He wanted no trouble. "Can you call the ambulance for me? Just look how swollen it is. Don't it look bad to you?"

"I can't say that I would know, mister," the man said, looking at the leg and then looking away. "I ain't no doctor, and I can't do nothing until Chief Acorn comes back. He won't be happy with me if I up and let you go. Besides, he might wanna talk with you about something else, like all the break-ins we been havin' 'round here. You know about that, do you? He's got a big investigation going on right now."

"I am no thief," Black Horse said, now getting plenty annoyed with the man and not caring that he showed anger. "I didn't commit no crimes, unless getting run over by a car is doing something wrong."

"We smelled liquor on you, Indian. We could keep you for drunkenness."

It was a weak threat, since Black Horse had been found outside of Mission and on tribal land. Mission authorities had no jurisdiction there, although sometimes they responded to emergency calls when they were south of Mission and on the Valentine Road.

"Of course that's up to the chief to say. But we could hold you easy enough."

Black Horse gave up talking to the man. He lay back and waited for the chief to return. He didn't know Chief Acorn very well. He couldn't actually remember the man by face, although Black Horse had been in the Mission Town jail once or twice over the years, but Acorn had a reputation for being fair—a reasonable man, somebody had described him once.

He thought some more about that coyote. Damned if it didn't seem to him like the critter came right up to him and all but said hello. If it was a dream or shock or something it was damn vivid, and the strangest kind of dream he had ever had. He wished his dad were still alive, for he often had good explanations of the unexplainable. But then, maybe there wasn't anything to explain. Perhaps it had been his imagination or a dream or shock or something else. But it sure did seem real to him.

About an hour later the chief came in, and when he got a look at Black Horse's leg he put in a

17

call for the tribal ambulance over at Rosebud. Acorn almost said something to his deputy about the importance of looking over prisoners' physical needs and then taking appropriate action. Then he decided to be quiet. To say anything would only embarrass the deputy, especially if what he said was said in front of the Indian. He couldn't afford to lose another deputy. It was hard enough to keep help as it was.

Acorn was as small as the deputy was large. He was about five feet five and weighed at the most 140 pounds. He wore cowboy boots and a cowboy hat and liked brightly colored shirts with rope ties. He was in his early forties and had a creased leathery-looking face that made him look like he had done his share of chasing cows on cold windy days. He had, too.

"So what the hell happened out there?" he asked.

Acorn brought Black Horse hot coffee and sat with him in the cell, the door open while they waited for the ambulance from Rosebud.

"The man who found you, Jeb Grablander, he said there was a coyote out there watching over you like a sentry. Those were his words. The strangest thing he ever seen, he said. He was sure you were a goner."

So I wasn't dreaming, Black Horse thought.

18

"You say the man saw the coyote standing near where I was found?"

It was an unusual incident and the chief wanted to know what the Indian felt had gone on. Some of the goddamn Indians he had in his jail could be so mysterious about these things. It plain pissed him off when they acted that way, but Black Horse didn't seem like the type.

"Did you see the coyote out there? What the hell you doin' so far out of Mission at that time of the mornin'? You break down and have to walk or somethin'? We didn't find any car, unless it drifted over. We got quite a load of snow out of this storm."

Black Horse shook his head. There was no car. He hadn't broken down, he explained. But he wasn't sure he wanted to say more than that. What was there to tell? Some distrustful bastard had dumped him. Left him to die. The rest he would keep to himself. The part about the coyote.

Chief Acorn could see that the man wasn't going to talk. He slammed the cell door shut and told his deputy to call again for the tribal ambulance from the Rosebud Hospital. He wanted to get rid of this Indian.

19

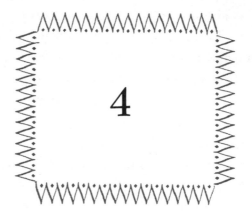

4

BLACK HORSE had a broken leg. The break wasn't
serious, though. The doctor called it a hair-line
fracture that required a small, lightweight cast.
Nothing more. The pain he felt in his back came
from a large bruise near his spine, but there was no
permanent damage. He had been lucky. Had the
injury been a couple of inches to one side he might
not be able to walk.

Once he got back to Corn Creek he tried to
forget the coyote and the walk in the snowstorm for
a while, even his waking up in the Mission Town
jail.

Everybody was happy to have him home and no one more so than Jim Bennion, the Mormon.

"I was some worried about you out in that storm," he said to Black Horse. "I had a feeling you had got caught out in it."

Bennion studied Black Horse, trying to determine if anything was different about the man. He was as usual, lighter after a stay in the Rosebud jail, but that came from the meager amounts of food served the prisoners. But this time there was a reserve about Black Horse that wasn't there after other stays in jail. Usually he was talkative, with lots of stories about what went on inside. But not now. And he hadn't asked about the lady from Rapid City, Mrs. Lindholm. Bennion expected her any day now. He had, in fact, expected her a few days earlier. She was coming to examine Black Horse's paintings for a showing in Rapid City, maybe.

Jim Bennion was a Mormon missionary on the reservation, although being a Mormon on an Indian reservation hadn't exactly been as easy as he had thought it would be. For one thing, he wasn't ready for the hostility, bordering on hatred, that came from the other churches on the reservation, but especially from the Jesuit fathers. They were downright vicious in their attitude toward Mormons. In part he understood the reason why, because the first Mormons who came to this particular reservation about a dozen years before had been overzealous. They went around telling the Jesuit fathers and the other missionaries that there were in fact only two churches in this world, the Mormon Church and the church of the Devil (all other churches). That wasn't exactly the way to bring people together, any fool knew, or to make new friends, but Mormons wanted converts, not friends. And the almost complete lack of a sense of humor by the young elders didn't help either. Unusually intense and somber they were, and that didn't make for easy living for anyone. But on an Indian reservation, where people liked to laugh even if the laugh was at their own expense, life could get a bit intense. And there was, too, the way the Mormons dressed. Quite formal. Ties always, and as often as not suit jackets even on the hottest of days when the temperatures would climb over 100°.

Mormon missionaries always were sent out in pairs, but Jim Bennion was alone in Corn Creek. He was the exception, although his situation was certain to be temporary.

Aside from living alone—and that wasn't his fault—Bennion might have been described as something of an unorthodox Mormon. From the Indians' point of view, for example, he was different in that he got on unusually well with the local people and understood and accepted the Indians' ways quite readily. He was not especially judgmental in that Mormon way, or for that matter, the way of all missionaries. On the other hand, as a missionary— which he was, after all, and was why he was supposed to be out there—he was a dismal failure. He had not made one convert since arriving on the reservation six months before, and in the eyes of the leadership of the Mormon Church that made his activities suspect.

Bennion had grown up Mormon, had known most of his life he would be going on a mission experience someplace, yet he had little of that aggressiveness that made for good missionaries. He just wasn't direct like the other Mormons on the reservation, nor anywhere near as pious.

He told Black Horse how he had known since he was a child that he would be a missionary and that his father, whom he called Pappy, had hoped he would choose an American Indian mission. It would have been possible for him to go anyplace, for Mormons were everywhere in the world, including South America, Asia, and Africa. But his pappy convinced him there was a lot that needed doing among American Indians and so much for him to learn from his Indian brothers. He listened and decided on an Indian mission, and he liked to tell how this decision had made his father proud.

The house in which Jim Bennion lived in Corn

Creek was large and well-lighted, although in other ways it was fairly primitive. There was no indoor bathroom or running water, but otherwise it was quite comfortable. The room was actually the back part of the community's meeting hall that once had served as a variety store and now was leased by the town from the Roman Catholic Church. And from what Bennion learned later, after he had rented the room from the community chairman, Lester Leader Charge, and had moved in, the priest in Corn Creek, Father Lane, had literally jumped up and down in anger when he was informed that the community leaders were actually providing housing to a Mormon elder. But there was little the priest could do besides complain. Later, when he discovered how poor a missionary Bennion was, he liked the arrangement more, an arrangement that made him some money too, for the community offered to share the rent they received from the Mormon. Half of sixty dollars. The priest could get very philosophical about the entire subject of Mormons, explaining to the other priests at St. Andrews that if he had to have a Mormon in his town, and it looked as if they all did, it was best he got a lazy missionary and not one of the go-getters and pushy types the other fathers had to deal with. Just about any of the other priests would happily have swapped Mormons with Father Lane.

"I should have knowed better," Black Horse said. "Knowed better than to get in with people from Pine Ridge. I was drunk and they seemed all right to me. I trusted them, Jim, and did I wish I hadn't a little while after. Never again, though. Never again will trust one of those Pine Ridgers." That was all he said about the incident, although wild stories about the coyote that followed Black Horse crisscrossed the reservation.

But Black Horse didn't tell anyone in Corn Creek about what happened, although he was being asked all the time. He said nothing. He had started to explain it all to his mother one night, but Doris Mae barged in at the wrong moment and, being a little drunk, she began to ridicule what he was saying. She said she thought he had been drunk and had imagined the entire episode or that he was making it up to get attention for himself. He damn near smashed her when she said this, but instead, he stopped talking and left. He knew that would anger Doris Mae more than anything else he could do, for she actually wanted to hear everything about the adventure, probably more than his mother did. Doris Mae was jealous that she hadn't been there herself. And that he had had this experience without her.

Black Horse lived with his mother and his sister and her husband and in-laws aplenty, and of course Doris Mae, who was his common-law wife. He had been with her now for more than six years. Ten people in all sometimes lived in that one-room shack in the northeast corner of Corn Creek near the edge of the dried-up creek bed that was used as a community dump. The once beautiful area had become a sea of trash and, no doubt, rats galore.

It was a couple of more days before Black Horse got back to work on his paintings. He had left several uncompleted when he was arrested and jailed. He had an understanding with Bennion that allowed him to use Bennion's room as a studio to work in. Bennion welcomed the company, especially in the evening when they had time to talk and share stories after the hall was closed and there was nobody else around to talk with.

5

SPRING CAME early that year. In April, what snow there was had melted. The sun warmed and thawed the prairie and every day a larger spread of green grasses covered the landscape.

As he had done all winter through, Black Horse continued to work on his paintings in Bennion's room, although there was another interruption in his work for a five-day stay in the Rosebud jail after he got drunk one night and threatened to beat up Doris Mae. This time his mother called in the tribal police and had him arrested and carried off to the lockup at Rosebud. He got the usual sentence, ten dollars or ten days. Since he didn't have the ten dollars, he would have to stay the ten days. At least that was what Bennion heard via the moccasin telegraph, his usual source of information. He didn't look to see Black Horse for another week and was surprised when one morning he heard a light tap on his door and found Black Horse's sister, Victoria, standing on his doorstep.

She was a young woman of an age difficult to determine. Maybe in her early twenties but she could have been older. She was very shy and spoke in a tiny voice, saying she was there to bring a message, and that message was that her brother's mother, Helen Black Horse, wished to see him right away and could he come? Before he could answer that he would be there right away, she was gone.

"I will be there right away," he called after her, but he was sure she couldn't hear what he said.

It took only five minutes to get to the Black Horses' place down back by the dump. When he got to the shack he found Helen Black Horse sitting on a mattress placed on a dirt floor in the middle of the room. The house was damp, even though the day was warm and sunny. It certainly wasn't the kind of housing for an old woman with bad arthritis. But he knew it was all she had and likely all she would ever have. If she wasn't there, where would she be? She was at least with people who cared about her, and that counted for a lot. As he went into the house he looked into the junk car in the yard. This was where Lyle Two Teeth was supposed to live. Black Horse had told him about Lyle and how strange a fellow he was. He was married to Victoria. What made him different was that he seldom spoke to anyone in the house except for Victoria, nor did he go into the house very often either. He lived in the car all year round. To Bennion the car didn't look like it would run, or, if it did, it wouldn't go very far, for two of the tires were flat and looked as if they had been flat for a long time. The rubber was actually rotting off the wheels. There was no one in the car now.

The house was nothing more than two low-roofed former chicken coops attached together. The large yard around it was enclosed by a broken-down poultry-wire fence. A driveway had been made where a portion of the fence had collapsed. At the front door lay an old car seat. It served in warm weather as an outdoor couch, although it probably hadn't been planned that way. More likely it was just dumped in that spot and left there.

"Elijah, he got sent to jail in Rosebud. You know this, Jim Bennion?" Helen Black Horse asked.

He did. The old woman spoke in a quiet voice

and very slowly, as if unsure of her words in English. She smiled, showing gray-black teeth with several missing in front. Her face was very wrinkled. She could barely stand. Bennion had no idea how old she was but he suspected she was younger than she looked. He had never heard Black Horse say how old she was. In spite of her inability to get around very well, she was very alert and she was without a doubt the decision maker in this home. Bennion knew this and so did everybody else, including Black Horse. She had the last word even when it meant having somebody put in jail. It wasn't the first time she had had to have her son arrested and she didn't expect it would be the last time either. She didn't say any of this to Bennion, however.

"Elijah, he was real crazy-acting the other night," she said. "Drinking too much." She smiled, but the smile was forced. She didn't feel like smiling. What had happened had not been funny. Bennion could see she was quite uncomfortable around him, but at the same time she trusted him. Not because she knew he could be trusted, but because of what Elijah had said about him being a man who was straight with the Indian people. "Jim Bennion can be trusted," he had told her. He had told her if she had trouble he could be depended upon to help out. She also accepted this without question. She would believe it if Elijah said it was so.

Doris Mae was there too. She didn't say anything, but Bennion guessed the cut across her eye was the result of a fight with Black Horse.

"I asked you to come here, Jim Bennion, because I want for you to go to Rosebud and pay Elijah's fine so he can come home. They charge me ten dollars to let him come home."

She produced a ten-dollar bill, folded neatly. It had been tucked in her shoe.

Again she smiled. She waited for his reaction. Would he do this thing for me? she thought.

"Sure sure," he said. "I don't mind going, not at all. I need to get into Rosebud soon anyway." That was a lie, really. He only hoped he could get to Rosebud and back without being seen by one of the other Mormons. They would want to know why he didn't go to the main church if he went to Rosebud. He wouldn't have a satisfactory answer.

"Besides, that lady from Rapid City is coming around any day now. Elijah ought to be here to meet her. She might not understand if he isn't."

The old woman said nothing to this. She didn't know what he was talking about, for Black Horse had said nothing to her about any lady coming to see him. Bennion could see this right away. He decided to be quiet about Mrs. Lindholm. He wouldn't say anything about the planned art show. He would leave that up to Black Horse. But Doris Mae heard what he said and was about to say something, but then she looked over at the old lady and for some reason said nothing.

"He's in Rosebud jail, isn't he?" Bennion asked, feeling stupid after asking such a question. Where else would he be? Everybody arrested on the reservation was taken to the jail at Rosebud. The old woman ignored his question.

That sure was a dumb question I asked, he said to himself as he walked back toward his room, fingering the ten-dollar bill in his pants pocket. In a way he hadn't wanted to take the money from Helen Black Horse, knowing how much she must have needed it. But he couldn't afford to be paying fines for Black Horse or any other Indian either. Besides, if it got around, like to the other Mormons, that he was paying for drunk Indians to get out of jail, well, all hell might break loose. The others would demand to know what he was doing paying fines for Indians. It never set quite right with him that others could be so critical about how he spent his own money. It wasn't as if the Mormon Church paid for his stay out there or, for that matter, of any of the others either. His father paid the bills, as did the families of the other elders. That was the understanding. That was part of the mission experience. Then, too, the jailings for Black Horse had been so frequent in recent months he couldn't have afforded helping in any meaningful way. He smiled when he thought about old Helen Black Horse. She sure made a good try when it came to keeping Black Horse out of the jail at Rosebud. He bet half of her monthly social security lately had gone for fines to get him out of jail.

After lunch he would leave for Rosebud.

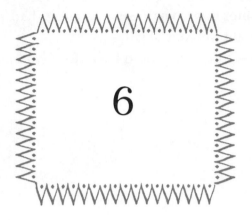

6

THE ROSEBUD JAIL is located next to the old com-
modity building, a stone building recently reno-
vated into offices for use by the tribe and various
government-sponsored programs. Bennion didn't
know what was in there now. Some kind of housing
administration offices, he had heard. This entire
complex of buildings, including the jail, was across
the street from the main tribal offices, a building
that looked to him very much like an elementary
school, with everything low and close to the
ground the way schools are built now. One floor

34

and sprawled out. The tribal office was next to the Bureau of Indian Affairs building that had been put up in the last century. It was three stories and looked like a dormitory at an old Eastern college or university.

The jail wasn't large but it was modern and efficient, perhaps the most efficient facility on the reservation. Like most everything, it was built by the federal government. The security at the jail was not tight. It didn't have to be, for most of the prisoners were in for drunkenness or petty theft or minor assaults. Serious crimes that happened on the reservation were tried off the reservation in a federal court. For this reservation such trials were held at Rapid City or Pierre (the capital) and sometimes at Sioux Falls. Less serious offenses were handled locally by the tribal court system, with judges appointed by the tribal president, Amos Featherman, with approval of the tribal council.

The afternoon Bennion arrived to inquire about the release of Black Horse, Bony Featherman, brother of the tribal council president Amos, was on duty at the front desk. He operated the police radio, answered the calls, and sent out the messages to the patrol cars (there were four for the entire reservation). He also met the walk-in traffic like Bennion who came to inquire about the prisoners.

Bennion liked Bony, although he considered him something of a talkative fool. He always had something to say. He was a tall, good-looking half-breed who, according to the rumors, was a woman chaser, although he was very much married and with two or three children. Sometimes Bennion thought he would have liked to ask Bony about the stories just to piss him off, but he wouldn't have dared now. The man might get angry and take it out on Black Horse.

"What can I do for you, Mr. Bennion?" Bony asked, smiling and friendly as he saw Bennion standing at the desk. He smiled a grin that said he knew why the Mormon was in this day. He was writing something on a yellow-lined note pad.

"He's a loser. He will never change. Drunks never do. You preachers come around and think you will change things, but you won't. You can't. They just make suckers of you. Use you. Then, when you wise up or get mad and say no more help, they go on to the next sucker. We have a real turnover of preachers out here. There are usually plenty of suckers, a new crop every few months. All come to save us poor Indians. Why? We go through more missionaries that way." He grinned.

"Look, Bony, save it, will you? His mother asked me to come and get him out. She gave me ten dollars to pay the fine. Look!" He produced the ten-dollar bill.

Bony thought about that for a moment as if trying to decide whether he believed Bennion.

"Well, I suppose she would give him her money if she had it, but I don't believe she has it to give, not now, anyway. I think you're buying him out again, Elder.

"You just don't want it to get around, right? You don't want those other elders finding out. No sir, they wouldn't like it a bit if they knew. You would catch hell from them sure enough. But don't worry, I can keep a secret." He winked and grinned some more. "So why don't you own up? You're paying his way out. Right?"

"Anything you say, Bony, but I tell you Helen Black Horse gave me the money."

Bony made out a slip of paper and went to the back where the jail is, but he came right back grinning more than ever.

"Ten bucks won't do it this time, Elder. I should have thought but I didn't. Plumb slipped my mind. It is twenty dollars this week.

"You see, your friend there got himself a charge of resisting arrest on him too. He put up a fight when Abe LaPointe picked him up. You will have to come up with another ten or he stays here."

37

"Okay, Bony. I will pay the difference. You're right after all, it seems. I have to pay his way out."

Black Horse of course was very happy to be out and somewhat surprised that he was being released so soon. He had known about the resist charge and knew it meant a higher fine. He hadn't expected anyone to come around to buy him out. Ten dollars his mother might have, but certainly not twenty.

From the jail Bennion and Black Horse went to the coffee shop, which was mostly empty then. The lunch crowd had gone back to their offices across Rosebud Creek. Rosebud was not only the home of the Bureau of Indian Affairs agency but the Public Health Service and Hospital as well, and just about everybody who didn't carry a lunch to work came to this coffee shop. There was no other place in Rosebud.

They sat at a card table with a metal surface with Coca Cola printed across the top and talked about the lady from Rapid City, Mrs. Lindholm. Bennion was telling Black Horse how she hadn't yet arrived and what a good thing that was, since Black Horse had been away. Black Horse gave Bennion some of his ideas about what paintings they should show the woman when she finally did arrive at Corn Creek. As he spoke he recognized someone he knew sitting at a table behind them.

He waved and hollered and the man looked up and returned the wave.

"Roger, what's you doing here?" Black Horse said. "I heard you give us up for Nebraska?"

Roger was a white man. He got up from the table where he sat with two Indian men, one of whom Bennion recognized as the tribal president himself, Amos Featherman, and came over to where they sat and shook hands with Black Horse. He was tall, so tall in fact that he couldn't get his legs under the card table without picking it off the floor. He dressed like a cowboy going to town, with a Western hat and cowboy boots carefully polished. They were not work boots. The man was about forty, perhaps a little older. He was not heavy, just tall and stringy.

"I can only stay a second," he said, speaking softly. He nodded at Bennion. Black Horse did not introduce him.

"I am here doing a bit of business with Amos and Leon," He looked toward the tribal president and the other man, Leon Little Sack, a tribal employee.

"I still lease sections of land over by St. Francis. I keep saying I'm going to put a few head of cattle out there someday but I never do. But I keep the land. It comes pretty cheap."

The man's full name was Roger Desmet. He

owned a ranch south of the reservation in a town named Gordon, across the line in Nebraska. Gordon was closer to the Pine Ridge Reservation than it was to Rosebud. The ranch had belonged to Desmet's wife's father and came to them when old Jesse Abnor died three years before. Before working the Gordon ranch, however, Roger had leased Indian land for a few years on the reservation. His small place was near Mission Town, and for one summer five or six years before, Black Horse had worked the ranch with Roger. He had been a good employer, Black Horse remembered.

"Look, Elijah, I will get right to the point. I've got a lot of work on my place and not much in the way of good help." He had no help. "How would you feel about coming to work for me again this spring? I could fix up one of the buildings in the back of my place and it could make a mighty comfortable house for you and your family. You could move over about April or May and work all summer, into the fall if you want. Like I say, I got plenty of work. Can't promise to pay a fortune but I will do good by you. Best I can."

Black Horse apparently didn't need time to think about this offer. He accepted the proposal right away. This surprised Bennion somewhat, while at the same time making him a little unhappy in that he didn't know what the accepting of this

40

job would do to their plans for the art show in Rapid City scheduled for late April or early May.

Roger wrote out his phone number and directions to his ranch and rushed off to finish his conversation with the tribal president, a man who didn't like to be kept waiting.

It wasn't until the drive back to Corn Creek that Black Horse said more about the move to Gordon and about why he was leaving the reservation. He acted as if he needed to explain the suddenness of his decision. Bennion wasn't looking for an explanation and was about to say so, but Black Horse wanted to talk about his plans.

"Roger Desmet is a damn good man to work for. Very fair. What is better is that I can get away from here for a while. I mean from living on the reservation. I can get Doris Mae and the kids out of my mother's house—not that there is so much wrong living there 'cept for the space and there is a lot of trouble. Too much drinking and fighting, I guess." He smiled as if what he said was an understatement, and it was. "I need a place where I can find hard work and not drink. In Gordon, at Desmet's place, it will be like that. He knows Indians real good. He will keep me from drinking. He's no fool. I need that now. And maybe I will get a chance to do a lot of good painting for a big show in Denver or someplace like that after the show in

Rapid City next month." That was the first he said to indicate that he wasn't abandoning the Rapid City show.

"You know, I need to do the paintings. For me it is like telling a story. A true story. I want to get something down on canvas that is honest, real, and maybe shows things how they are around here 'cept everything changes so dum fast that what is true one day is wrong the next. You know what I am saying? I think the old way is being bulldozed away. Just like the way they cut through the hill to make that Grass Mountain Road."

They were then passing through the Ghost Hawk Park where the Indian Affairs road crews were cutting down trees and widening the road to make it straighter and in so doing were ruining much of the beauty of the ride through Ghost Hawk Park. The year before, the crews had carved a wide swath through Grass Mountain and connected it with Spring Creek. It, too, destroyed a lot of beautiful land along the Little White River.

"Maybe if we go away, Doris Mae and me will get along more. Being on Desmet's place might be good for us. Might get to save a little money too, and next winter when we come back we will get us a place of our own. Maybe a house with a couple or three rooms and electricity so I don't have to bother you with all my paints and canvas boards."

"It isn't any bother," Bennion said. "I told you that before." He meant it, too, but he understood Black Horse's wish to have a place of his own. It made sense, just as the move to Gordon now began to make sense. He would miss his friend but he was glad he was going. The business of Black Horse being in and out of the Rosebud jail was getting old anyway, Bennion thought.

They were coming out of the Ghost Hawk Park. The dark shapes of the ponderosa pines were behind them now and lighter grass of the flatter land ahead stretched out. From here on in, and for the next forty miles, the land was flat. Corn Creek was built on a flat parcel of land with no trees for cover from the hot summer sun or a buffer from the cold winter winds. On a knoll off to the left were the tiny wooden crosses of a cemetery. It sure was a lonely spot.

They weren't back in Corn Creek more than a couple of hours when Bennion saw a government vehicle pull into his drive. He guessed it was Mrs. Lindholm. He sent a boy to find Black Horse, who came right away. He arrived somewhat breathless, as if he had run all the way from his mother's place.

Mrs. Lindholm was a gray-haired woman in her late fifties. She was a bit stout and very businesslike, while at the same time pleasant. She took in the room in a glance, seeming to understand that

43

this was where the artist Black Horse did most of his work. She understood the arrangement. She knew very well how bad Indian housing was on most reservations. She went over to a couple of Black Horse's paintings that were partially completed. Most of the finished canvases were stacked in the adjoining room.

"I take it you have enough of these for the show," she said, speaking to no one in particular. Black Horse said that he did. He offered to bring out his supply of completed works but she declined the opportunity to see more.

She spoke slowly, enunciating each word carefully. Her accent wasn't Western, although Bennion had heard she had lived in South Dakota for many years. Maybe most of her adult life.

"And you can get to Rapid City okay?" she asked, turning to face Black Horse for the first time.

Black Horse looked at Jim Bennion for the answer. It would be Bennion who would drive them to Rapid City. He had said he would.

"But of course," Black Horse said at last. He acted very confident, while Bennion was less sure. Not because he wouldn't be willing to drive the two hundred miles to Rapid. That wasn't it at all. It was that he wasn't confident something wouldn't happen before the show. Something like Black Horse getting jailed again. But he didn't say this to the woman. How could he say that their coming depended on Black Horse remaining sober?

It was almost as if she read his mind, when she said, "I am fairly strict about one thing."

Here it comes. Bennion thought.

"And that's... well, drinking. I don't want my artists coming to Rapid City drunk, nor do I want them drinking while the show is on. Shows generally last about four days. Is that understood?"

She looked right at Black Horse and then to Jim Bennion. It was as if she were trying to decide how bad a drinking problem this one had. She hadn't dealt with many Indians, artists or not, who didn't or hadn't had a problem with booze. It was simply a matter of degree with her. If the man could remain sober for the four-day show, she didn't give a damn what he did after that.

"I will be frank. I don't much like to become involved with artists who can't control their liquor. It simply doesn't work out, for me or for them."

She just wasn't again going to be embarrassed by some drunken fool running around her gallery and offices causing trouble.

Changing her mind, she asked to see a couple of completed canvases and seemed satisfied that the quality of the work was okay for her show. But she wasn't exactly excited by what she saw either. Indeed, she acted a bit bored. She had seen work by this man before. He painted well enough, she thought, in a technical sense, but he wasn't special, at least she didn't think he was. Like many others, he liked to copy pictures he saw in books and magazines, and she didn't consider that art, not real art. The truth was that she didn't often see much in the way of paintings by Indians that she thought was very good or original. Most of it, she thought, had been slapped on canvas to satisfy tourists and at the same time get a little money for liquor.

But one of Black Horse's paintings did interest her. She perked up when she saw it and asked if there might be more ready in time for the show.

It was another landscape, but different from the others. Unfinished, it depicted a man in a snowstorm with an animal lurking behind him at some distance. The way the man stood made her feel as if he knew the animal was behind. She thought it was a wolf following behind him.

"Now, this one is quite good," she said.

Black Horse smiled. He was pleased.

"I hope you will finish it. It has a calm and mysterious mood about it. I like it very much." She smiled for the first time and seemed to relax. She looked at Black Horse more carefully now, wondering for a moment if this man might be better at what he did than the usual artist she dealt with. She hoped so.

And with that she excused herself, saying something about an appointment with the tribal president at Rosebud and how she was already late and she had heard he didn't like to be kept waiting.

How right you are, Bennion thought. Amos doesn't like to wait for anyone, but he thought nothing about making others wait for days to see him. Bennion knew, for he had had to wait for more than half a day once to get to see President Featherman, and for something that could have been dealt with by a subordinate, except Amos liked to keep all decisions, big or small, in his own hands. Tribal politics were like that.

7

IN SPITE OF THE carefully formulated plans for the art show in Rapid City set for late in April, two days before the opening of the show Bennion had to call Mrs. Lindholm and cancel out, much as he hated the unpleasant chore. Black Horse was in jail, he told her. She said nothing. He didn't explain what had happened. She wouldn't want to know the details anyway. She mumbled something about understanding how these things occur and said maybe the show might be rescheduled, but Bennion knew it never would be.

Bony Featherman had been right, Bennion thought with annoyance bordering on anger. He could see the son of a bitch grinning smugly when they carried in Black Horse.

By the time Black Horse got out of jail, ten days had gone by. Nobody bought him out this time. The days were warm now almost hot, some of them, and the land was a vast ocean of green, dotted with multicolored wild flowers as far as the eye could see.

The grass often stays green until the summer sun turns the land brown as early as July, if the year is dry as it had been for the past three years—drought years, all of them.

In jail for the eighth time that winter, Black Horse had ample opportunity to think, and it was here that he made his final decision that it was indeed time for him to leave the reservation for a while.

Bennion believed this too. Maybe the hard ranch work would be good for Black Horse. It ought to keep him sober. Surely he couldn't drink and keep a job with Desmet. And Desmet was sure to do all in his power to keep Black Horse far away from the liquor. It was very much in his own interest that he did. In everybody's interest, in fact.

Bennion helped Black Horse pack, piling everything, which wasn't very much, into several cardboard boxes. Mostly it was canvas boards and paints and cans he kept his brushes in.

As they packed they talked, but not about the art show canceled at Rapid City. That was done, and Black Horse felt no need to go over it again. And Bennion wouldn't bring up the subject if the Indian didn't. Black Horse didn't even ask Bennion if he had been in contact with Mrs. Lindholm in Rapid. He knew he had. Bennion was like that.

They didn't talk about anything very important. Instead, it was about things going on in Corn Creek. What the local Catholic priest was up to in the way of trying to be rid of Elder Bennion.

"Is he still trying to put you out from this room?" Black Horse asked with a grin. "You watch out for Father Lane. He don't much like other preachers, but especially he don't like Mormons. I ever tell you about the time he got mad at me when I had our last baby baptized with Father Burger?" Father Burger was an Episcopalian.

He had. Twice before. But that didn't keep him from telling the story again. Explaining how he had been drinking that day and got a bit confused and Father Burger was around and willing to do the baptismal and did. When Father Lane heard about it, he was furious. Furious at Black Horse but equally angry at the Episcopal priest. According to what Black Horse told, the two priests hardly spoke to each other even yet, and all because of this misunderstanding a few years before.

Black Horse was about to leave now. He shook hands with Bennion and said, "I know this will be right for me, Jim. Going to Gordon is good." He picked up a box to carry out to the car that was waiting for him. Then he put it down and said, as if remembering something important, "You know, for all the times I've been in jail here and other places away from the reservation, I ain't never got so low or hard up that I ever took to begging like you see some Indians do in Rapid City. Nope, I've not got that far down, Jim, but if I don't get far from here a while I will."

He laughed and said, "I ain't got so low that I took to drinking cheap rot-gut wine either." With that comment he was gone, gone south to Nebraska for the summer.

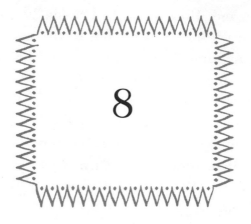

8

ROGER DESMET watched the car as it came through his gate. It was an old car and noisy. An Indian car, for sure. He couldn't tell what make it was, but it was big. Probably a Pontiac or a Buick. And it was dirty, covered with mud so he couldn't see the color. Maybe green, maybe brown or black, even. He wasn't sure. Indians liked big cars and white car dealers liked to sell the gas hogs to Indians. The ones nobody else wanted. Everybody was happy, at least for a while until the clunkers began to fall apart, as they almost always did. About the only plus for the cars, Roger thought, was that being large like they were provided more protection than smaller Chevrolets or Fords, and the Indians needed all the protection they could find, for they were often involved in the god-awfulest fiery multiple-car crashes a person might imagine. Eight or nine people could die in a bad Indian car wreck. This way at least they had more protection with the big cars.

Black Horse had called the day before to say he would be coming to Gordon today, but Desmet hadn't really expected him for a day or two more. He understood Indian time very well—too well, he thought. His being on time was good, though. It meant the man was serious about coming to work for him. The next day was Monday and they could begin a new week together. Start off everything in the right way.

The house in back was ready and had been ready for several weeks.

He could see three, no four, maybe five people in the car that was almost to the top of the driveway now. By habit he looked over at his gun rack, which was locked to keep the kids out of it. But it wouldn't take him very long to get out a shotgun or rifle if he needed it fast.

The Indian-white trouble in the region that year had his wife, Joanne, plenty nervous about inviting an Indian family to live on the place. She told him she feared they might begin to have pow-wows and parties and invite their reservation families and friends over and that trouble would follow. He wasn't sure she was wrong. Anything was a possibility, but he didn't expect that to happen with Black Horse. Unless the man had changed a great deal, and he hadn't seemed to when he saw him at Rosebud. Except for one small problem with drinking a few years before when he had Black Horse working for him, everything went along fine that year.

If only he didn't have to be away so much of the time he would feel better about having the Indians on the place for the summer. If he were around more he could keep a watch on things, but this was not possible because he was a part-time agricultural extension agent for the county. That meant he was hired to help other ranchers in the area with their problems, mostly problems caused by the drought. Because of the dry weather, however, he was required to be on the job more hours each week, which was turning this part-time job into something approaching full time. But he needed the money. As it was, Joanne was working too. She was a head-start teacher for the town of Gordon. They needed every cent she could earn.

What it all came down to, like it or not, was that he had to trust Black Horse to work on his own without supervision, which, so long as the man didn't drink, would be no problem at all. Black Horse didn't need to be told what was expected of him. He was a self-starter. He did what was expected of him and then some.

But would he stay sober? That was the big question haunting Roger.

It was Black Horse and his family in the big car. He could see them clearly now. Black Horse was the first out of the car. He waved to Roger, who stood on his front step watching as the others got out too, and they began to unload the car in the front yard. Roger was about to signal for the man to drive around behind the main house but then he decided not to bother. There wasn't going to be all that much to carry. He could see that. Only looked like paper bags and cardboard boxes full of clothing.

When Roger got his first good look at Doris Mae he whistled a low whistle and muttered to himself, "My God." There was no one close enough to hear him. Doris Mae was skinny and looked sick to him. Not just sick, but diseased. She had brown hair, stringy matted hair that looked very dirty, as he was sure it was. It hadn't been washed in a very long time, he decided. It was almost caked on her head like sand that had dried in the sun. And she had no teeth, or so few that the ones she had didn't show.

Now he was down at the car helping to unload

the boxes. There were more than he had expected. It was hot standing in the sun and he wished he had told the fellow to drive around back. Doris Mae smelled, he noticed. The boxes smelled too. She unpacked the car without once looking at him, although he was sure she saw him walk to the car. Still, she didn't say so much as hello or even look in his direction or nod to him or anything to acknowledge that he was there or that he existed and that she had seen him.

What in the world had happened to his other wife? What was her name? He couldn't remember anymore. But she was nice and friendly and took good care of her kids and kept a clean house. She even liked coming up to visit with Joanne and having coffee with her. The two got on fine and Joanne wasn't all that fond of Indians. But this one—he didn't know about her. He had seen other women like her on the reservation before and they could be plenty of trouble. He hated to think how much trouble. She was one of those Indian women who wouldn't speak to a white man unless almost made to or when drunk, and then she'd often have a hell of a lot to say to white people and most of it not very friendly. He wished he had known about her before he invited Black Horse to move in. It might have made a difference, even though he couldn't see how it would. Desperate as he was for halfway good help for the summer, he didn't have many choices. Yet there was a limit.

Black Horse saw Roger's concern. He watched him studying Doris Mae. Probably trying to make a decision as to whether he ought to let us move onto his place. He knows already what she is like, and he's worried. He has reason to be concerned. But he would do what he could to reassure Roger first chance he got. Maybe tell him Doris Mae would be all right, though he wasn't entirely sure of that himself. She might be okay and she might not be. She could be funny-acting when she wanted to be. Mighty ornery too.

Black Horse stuck out his hand to Roger Desmet and said, "Good to see you again, my friend. We are on time, no?"

It hadn't been by accident that he was on time. He had planned it this way, figuring on surprising Desmet.

"Right you are and am I ever glad you are. We got plenty fixin' to do around here and tomorrow is not too soon to be getting at it."

He hadn't told Black Horse he would be working alone much of the summer, not that he thought the news would make any difference to the man. He was, in fact, confident it wouldn't matter at all. He would tell him later.

Roger and Black Horse walked ahead, each

carrying a large cardboard box. They walked toward the house down back.

Black Horse began right away to explain about Doris Mae. "She's okay, Roger. I know she don't look so okay, but she is. She's shy around white people. She ain't been far from the reservation too much so she's a little backward. You know what I mean?"

Desmet did know what he meant and it worried hell out of him, but he didn't say this.

Black Horse laughed a weak laugh and Roger tried to smile. Both were uncomfortable with the conversation.

We shall see, Roger thought. We will just have to wait and see.

"I hope you're right, Elijah, 'cause trouble around this place ain't something I need. With this drought and all the trouble from the Indians who came over from Rapid City this winter and wherever the hell else they come from, well, that's plenty. Those Indians aren't any people I ever met on the reservation, I know that much. I guess you heard about all the trouble?"

"Nobody talks about anything else on the reservation," Black Horse said.

"Same here too. Militant Indians and the dry weather. Each is about as welcome as snow in July. Sometime soon I figure it's gotta rain, but we said that last year and the year before that and we don't see much rain. It is awfully dry. You can see that."

Black Horse said nothing. He saw the condition of the ranch. And the land coming into Gordon—parched and nearly burned black. The man would be lucky to survive another year if there wasn't some relief. He felt sorry for Roger Desmet. He must be having one hell of a time making the place pay.

"There's one thing, I hope you don't mind my asking, Elijah. I mean it is none of my business I suppose but I am gonna ask anyway. What ever became of your other wife? I don't remember her name."

Black Horse looked down at the ground and kicked a stone. The dust rose, it was so dry underfoot.

"You mean Laurene," he said. "She's gone. Died one winter day about seven years ago. They said maybe it was TB, but I don't think so. She was gone so fast it could have been anything. She was sick about two weeks and then she was dead. A fine woman she was."

They spoke of other things as they made several trips back and forth to the cabin, but nothing more was said about Doris Mae. The house was a few yards beyond a small corral Desmet used to keep his horses in.

Black Horse had two children with Doris Mae, a girl about five years old and an infant, a boy, about seven or eight months old.

Doris Mae picked up the baby from a box that Roger had thought contained rags. He didn't know there was a baby in it. The baby was wrapped in a dirty blue blanket. It smelled like there was a need to change the diaper.

That's all I will need, Roger thought, is to have someone say the Indians on my place aren't taking good care of their kids.

The other woman, Laurene, he thought, would never have had a baby dressed like that. No matter how poor they were, the children were clean and looked good and were well kept. But this mother would be different. He could see that already.

The house he had made over for Black Horse had once been a large tool shed with one of those thin cement coverings on the outside walls. It was adobe-like in appearance, but actually it was cement with log construction underneath. It was a well-made building that promised to be hot in the summer, but tight and comfortable in winter. There wasn't much in the way of shade trees around the shed and the weather had been steaming hot although it was still early for such heat. The partitions he had put up made the shed into a fairly decent-sized three-room house. There was a kitchen, a bedroom, and a living room, and the furniture came from the barn. He had used things that had belonged to Joanne's father. The pots and pans and dishes were old ones Joanne no longer needed. There was running water but no indoor toilet. He had dug an outside privy in back of the place a good distance away. The refrigerator was filled with food, including a freezer that had several frozen chickens and small cuts of beef.

"Say hello to the white man," Black Horse said in Indian to his little girl, whose name was Denise. He laughed when she tried to pull away and hide behind his leg so she wouldn't have to look up at Roger Desmet. She laughed easily and often as Black Horse kept telling her to say hello to Roger. While he didn't frighten her and she was having fun, she had never in her life seen anybody so tall.

They were in the house now, and Doris Mae was with them. She dropped several paper bags on the kitchen floor. She still hadn't said a word in way of greeting to Roger. Nothing, not so much as a hello, and while he kept looking at her, trying to catch her eye, she would not look at him straight on.

Finally Black Horse introduced her to Roger, saying, "Roger, this is Doris Mae and my son, Robert. I call him Stinker Little Thing." He laughed when he said this and Roger smiled and he thought he saw Doris Mae smile.

"And you know Denise." She tried to hide again and then ran over to be near her mother.

Roger said hello straight at Doris Mae and this time there was no mistaking whom he was talking to. She looked in his direction for the first time and said hello and then looked down at the floor. She kept looking at the cement floor all the time she was there. She said nothing more and he tried to ignore her, but he was having a difficult time hiding his concern about the woman and her shy ways. Her quietness bothered him. It wasn't normal for a grown woman with two kids to be so withdrawn, even if she was a reservation Indian and shy around white people. He was hardly the first white person she had seen. She had to have gone to school some, and most of the teachers in the reservation schools were white. She ought to be capable of more communication than this.

"I believe you will like this place," he said at last, trying to pick up his spirits and stop thinking about this woman. "There's no inside bathroom yet, but give me a few months and there will be everything if all goes good this year. That's my plan, anyhow. I just didn't have the time." Nor did he have the money, but he didn't say this to the Indians.

"There's a fresh-dug privy in the back. I think you will find the house comfortable. Everything you need to cook with is here. And there is some food in the refrigerator to get you started. I know you have your own things, but I figured you could use some more."

He didn't know that at all. Joanne had been right in insisting he put some pots and pans and dishes in the place beforehand. They will come with nothing, she had told him. He didn't believe her and was worried about offending Black Horse's wife by stocking the house. He was wondering if somehow Joanne knew Black Horse was with a different woman. Now he could see it was a good thing they had done this, for there was next to nothing in the boxes. Only clothing that he could see. No supplies and no household items. It amazed him. Nobody bothered to say a word about what they would need or wouldn't need when they talked on the phone days before. If Joanne hadn't guessed what things would be like, the house might have been empty aside from the basic furniture.

Roger considered this house about as good as anything on the reservation, and better built and cleaner than about three quarters of what passed as adequate housing over there. But above all it wasn't crowded, and all their relatives weren't likely to be moving in with them here in Gordon. No ten or twelve people living in one or two rooms. And not on his place was he about to allow this to happen. That would be made clear if the family started to arrive. But he was fairly sure that Black Horse knew this basic rule. He had lived with white people enough times to know how they were.

Before returning to his house on the top of the knoll about a quarter of a mile away, he announced that everybody was invited to Sunday dinner at about three P.M. It was then about one P.M. He hoped Joanne wouldn't be too angry with him for not telling her. The idea came to him, popped in his head, as he was leaving Black Horse and family. He saw they might not have much for a dinner and it might be a good way to get things started right, to get everybody comfortable and free with one another. Those things were important, he knew.

It was still hotter when he left the shed and walked slowly up the hill to his place. The water windmill near the barn spun wildly in the strong wind and he thought again about climbing up on that windmill and tying down the wheel before it came free and took off on its own and did some damage or hurt stock. With the help of Black Horse he thought he might get that thing tied down the next morning. It felt good to him to have a bit of help around the place. Working a ranch alone wasn't easy in the best of times, and these weren't the best of times.

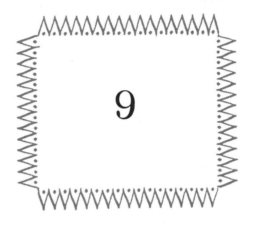

9

JOANNE DESMET was preparing dinner when he came in. He told her there would be company for dinner and then rushed for the bathroom to get away from her. He knew she would be right behind and that she wouldn't be very happy with him either.

"What do you mean, company?" she hollered at him through the door. "Who?"

"Guess," he said. He almost laughed, but he knew she was damn annoyed.

"Damn you, Roger," she said. Then she went

away. He knew she would make room for the Indians.

Joanne Desmet was a big woman. Big like Roger, although not as tall. But she had big bones, a big frame, and was pretty, or once had been, in that farm-girl kind of attractiveness found in places like Nebraska. Some people might call it wholesomeness. Four children and the hard work around the place had taken some of the glow out of her face and flattened her figure, but she was still attractive.

And, like Roger, she too had grown up near an Indian reservation and had the usual biases of white people who live near Indians. But she was much more open with her opinions than Roger. He was more guarded—he saw and dealt with a good number of Indians all the time. She didn't. Still, sometimes she believed he didn't share many of her views about Indians, although she didn't understand how that could be, considering that his experience had been about the same as hers when it came to Indians. He had seen the same things. But for some reason she didn't always understand, he could make excuses for their often erratic behavior. She respected his right to believe what he wished and even his defending what he believed in, but she sure didn't agree with him most of the time when it came to the subject of Indians. She didn't think she ever had.

When finally he came out of the bathroom she was waiting for him.

"I didn't like the looks of that woman with him. I suppose she is his latest wife. Whatever happened to the other wife?" She couldn't remember Black Horse's first wife's name either. It had been a lot of years. "I wonder where he found her?"

"I don't know. Why don't you ask him when he comes up?"

"I might, Roger. I just might," But he knew her better than that. She wouldn't dare. She didn't have the nerve or the bad manners.

"His first wife, she was so different. She was beautiful and she took good care of the kids. I wonder what became of those children? They wouldn't be grown yet. There were three of them —I remember that. And they are not the ones she has now. They wouldn't be that young. No, these are new ones, probably by this woman. Just look what it got his other wife going around with a guy like that. What's his name again? I can't remember. I guess I don't want to remember."

"Elijah, Elijah Black Horse," he said, annoyed that he was having to tell her again. This for about the third time that day.

"For God's sake, try to remember his name, Joanne. And let's not go over all of this again. You know they are going to be here all summer, so get used to it."

He knew she would quiet down soon, quiet down and accept the fact that the Indians were going to live on the place for the next few months. But not like it, though.

"But Roger, that woman looks sick to me. She really does. She looks like she might have TB or some other awful disease from that dirty reservation. Did you ever see anybody so skinny? You know those Indians get all kinds of diseases, some we never heard of, or least we don't hear of them today. I hope she isn't going to bring us sickness on top of everything else we got to worry on."

"Maybe she is just run down," Roger said. "Life on the reservation ain't easy, 'specially in the winter, and last winter was a hard one. And where they have to live is real tough. Ten people in not more than one or two rooms. Amos Featherman told me how they live out at Corn Creek, but he didn't need to tell me. I been around the reservation plenty."

Roger had tried to check out Black Horse with Amos Featherman. His response was a shrug of the shoulders and something about how he might work out about as well as the others he was recommending if... There was that big IF again.

"*Have* to live," she said. "They don't *have* to

live on that reservation and you know that as well as I do, Roger. Nobody is making them stay. Nobody's holding a gun on them. There is no way I would live out there. How long are we expected to put up with the way they like to live and to pay with our taxes, no less. It's gone on for years, since we were both children and before that, even.

"Nothing ever gets any better. Worse, maybe, if that is possible. Sometimes I wonder how anything could get much worse than life on an ugly Indian reservation. But please don't tell me they must live like that in all that filth. They can leave. A lot of them have. And live just like anybody else. Get a job like the rest of us have to do. But the truth is they don't want to leave. You know that. Nothing keeps them on that stupid reservation except the government's willingness to pay to keep the places open. They really ought to close down those...hell holes. That is what they are."

"You wouldn't look any better, Joanne, if you stayed out there for a couple winters." He was surprised at his own forcefulness. She did annoy him when she spoke in this way.

"That's the point. I wouldn't stay. You couldn't keep me there. That's the difference. I wouldn't be such a fool. I would find something better."

"Where would you go?"

"Where does anyone go? To the cities, I guess,

or even to a small town where I could find myself a little job and take proper care of my family."

"But who would have someone like Doris Mae? You don't even want her here for Sunday dinner."

"I didn't say that."

"You didn't have to. Your face said it."

He was right, she knew. She hadn't wanted Doris Mae or the others in her house for dinner. Not for dinner this Sunday or any other. But she didn't argue the point with him. She would have them for dinner, and whatever else was asked of her, if Roger did the asking and it would make things easier for him. But she wasn't going to suggest the idea. He would have to ask them himself. She wouldn't.

It was a few minutes before three when Black Horse came to the door. He was alone.

"Doris Mae," he explained, "she don't wanna come. You see, she is shy around white people. She's afraid she will do somethin' wrong."

He laughed, as if what he was saying was the most ridiculous thing he had ever heard.

"I told her you are good folks and won't watch what she does, but she won't change her mind. She can be stubborn like that. Maybe I can bring something back for her and Denise."

"Of course," Roger said, worry in his voice.

"There's plenty." There was plenty, too, but Joanne said nothing. She wasn't surprised. The more backward Indians like that one, Doris Mae, did things like this.

But Roger was concerned that something might be wrong, and so soon. "You sure she ain't sick?" he asked.

"No, she's fine. She's putting things away now. She's in one of her stubborn moods. You know, she is kind of slow. Oh, she is smart enough, but she is slow about things away from the reservation. Except for a trip to Mobridge once for a week 'bout two years ago and I took her up there, this is the first time she's lived away from the reservation in her life and she is almost twenty-eight now. 'Cept she lived for a spell on the Standing Rock Reservation." When she was married to one Feather, he thought, but he didn't say this to Roger.

Not yet twenty-eight. To Roger she looked more like fifty-eight.

"No good letting her peculiar ways spoil a good dinner now, is there?" He laughed again. Roger saw he was uncomfortable with the situation. But then, they all were uncomfortable with the situation. Just the same, Black Horse and Roger and Joanne and the Desmet's four children sat down to a very quiet Sunday dinner. Roger said later it was the quietest meal he had sat through since he had had children. The conversation was between Roger and Black Horse exclusively, with the children sitting in silence and on their very best behavior, more than a little intimidated by the Indian in their home. They had seen plenty of Indians and had heard all kinds of stories from their grandfather and others in school, but never had one actually sat at their table with them. Roger tried, unsuccessfully, to get them to talk, but they said nothing, nor did Joanne say anything. Her reasons were different, however. She wasn't intimidated. She simply felt she didn't have anything to say to this man except she would have loved to have asked him what became of his other children. But she would never have dared ask that.

The conversation between Roger and Black Horse was all business. What work needed doing around the place and in what order and what Roger would expect of his new hired man. There was a brief talk of wages, but what it came down to was that Black Horse trusted Roger to be fair, and he was.

Roger then explained how he would have to be away much of the summer and that Black Horse would be on his own. That information seemed not to bother the Indian at all. Roger watched Black Horse's face for a reaction. There was none. It was almost as if he expected such an arrangement, although he hadn't, but it didn't make any difference to him. He would do the work required of him and more, if necessary.

His job consisted of general chores around the place. Things like putting in new fence, repairs on the barn, hauling water and hay and whatever else came up.

10

FOR THE FIRST few days he worked alongside Roger
and soon he began to wonder if Roger might have
changed his mind and was going to stay with him
all the summer long. He said nothing about leaving
to do his county work, and Black Horse did not ask
him when he intended to leave. He figured the
man would tell him when the time was right.

For one entire day they dug holes for fence
posts and another day repaired the roof on the barn
and tied down the windmill. They talked much at
first, sharing stories about persons they both knew
on the reservation, some of them now dead.

At other times there were long stretches when neither man said much of anything to the other. Sometimes Black Horse thought Roger wanted to talk to him, maybe ask him about the trouble between whites and Indians that everyone else was talking about. But he didn't ask. He remained silent. Desmet was different from a lot of white men Black Horse knew. For one thing, he was unlike other whites in that he didn't have to be talking all the time. He could be silent for hours and not feel uncomfortable. But the subject of the recent tensions between whites and Indians hung there and it was only a matter of time, Black Horse thought, before they would be talking about it just like everyone else. He thought some about what he would say to Roger when the questions were asked. He knew his opinion was no more important than the next guy's, but he also knew he would be asked for an opinion if only because he was Indian and was thought to have some ideas that others in the Gordon area hadn't heard before. The fact that he didn't wouldn't matter very much. They would want to know what he thought anyway.

One day when they were fixing a piece of fence near the barn Roger asked straight out, which was his usual way of doing things. He didn't work around a subject. He came straight at it, head on. He had been silent for a long time and Black Horse had guessed he might be thinking about how to bring up the subject of militant Indians.

"So what do you make of the commotion we been having around here?" he asked. "I mean all them Indians coming in from Rapid City, the radical ones, and the threats they make and the talk of getting back at us white people, all that stuff. What do you think about it? What are they saying over at Rosebud? Just talk is it, or is there more trouble coming out of this?"

Black Horse stopped what he was doing. He smiled. Then the smile disappeared.

"Roger, I don't know no more than the next guy. Maybe less. And I sure don't know the people running this show. Now, come to think of it, I know one of them. The one they call Boneshirt. Not Robert. His brother, Edward. I know he's from Rosebud, and he was a pretty good fellow, too. Not any kind of troublemaker like the TV says. He went away about three years ago on a relocation program, to Chicago or someplace like that. Was going to be trained to work on the airline, I hear, as a ticket taker or something. Next thing I hear he is back in Rapid City and in the middle of this trouble along with his brother Robert, who is in charge of everything. Edward, when he was on the reservation, sure was a lot different." He smiled when he said this. "Then he was a big shot for some sort of tribal program and he had on a tie and jacket and he'd go to big restaurants off the reservation. I bet he drank a lot of good whiskey that the government paid for, too." He laughed again. "Just like the white man he was, but as I say he was a pretty good fellow. Now I see he has his hair braided and he goes into the sweat lodges and does Indian dances all the time. Why, I bet he don't even speak Indian good!"

Desmet knew the Boneshirt name. It put fear into many people in the territory because the older Boneshirt brother was, in his opinion, damn near crazy. He did insane, reckless things and didn't seem to fear at all for his own life or safety. Already several people had taken shots at him—whites, he supposed—and one nicked him in the arm with a knife in some bar outside of Rapid City. He was just plumb loco, but Desmet didn't say this to Black Horse. He would be polite.

"Well, what do you reckon they're after? And why the hell they coming over here to Gordon? I would think they would be doing their hell-raising on the reservation where most of the Indians live."

"Yeah, that do seem like the place to be, don't it?" Black Horse said. "What they want, I think, is power. Ain't that what all the groups want? Everybody in politics wants power, wants to run everything or everybody else. Ain't no different with

Indians. I try not to get involved in politics. I work at ranch work and I do my paintings. That's all. I don't have no time for more than that. So if you ask me how it is on the reservation, all I say is that it sure was quiet when I left and I think it will stay that way. But I don't know. Oh, we hear rumors. Plenty of them.

"One time I even heard the militants was going to take over the tribal office building and run off Amos Featherman. They don't like Amos, you know. Say he too much like a white man. Even dresses like one with his two-hundred-dollar suits, and that's true, I know. That proved to be just talk. But I don't think Amos was much worried about them threats. He knows the people at Rosebud real good. He's no fool.

"I can't see how this trouble will be good for us. Whites and Indians won't be better off for it, the way I see it.

"I guess there is something we should be learning from what is going on, but I'll be damned if I know what it is unless it is we should be getting along better and care about one another more and not always be so damn suspicious all the time."

Roger wished his wife could hear a bit of this. She might be surprised at what the Indian was saying.

"I heard one good story about what is going on.

I guess it is funny. There was this group of Indian people, some of them from Rosebud, who wanted to hold a powwow over near Wagner. This group had been having powwows in Wagner for maybe five-six years years, always the same time of year. So they shows up again this year and find Wagner locked up, locked up tight. I mean, not one store was open. Nobody around. Other years Indian people spend lots of money in Wagner and the shopkeepers they pretty happy to do business with Indians. Now they are all gone off like there was a holiday or they all decided to go fishing on the same day. One of the Indians went to see the mayor and says, 'Look here, Mr. Mayor, we is the same Indians who have been coming here for years with no trouble and there won't be no trouble this time either.' The mayor must've believed him for he made some calls and the town opened up just like that!" He snapped his fingers. "And the Indians got what they needed and the shop people was happy to sell things."

"It is just about that bad in Valentine now," Roger said. "People there are getting ready for trouble. They figure they've been missed and that it isn't likely to continue. I think they're right, too. This kind of trouble spreads. Nobody gets off without a little action. They are mighty nervous over there, I can tell you that."

So that explained why their jail was full of reservation Indians. And that was also the reason they
let him off early. They didn't want to keep him for
fear they would need his space for the real trouble-
makers. They didn't want any more Indians than
they had to have, and so the harmless ones like him
got let off without so much as a hearing in front of
the judge. The drunks they would let go home, but
the militants, if they could be picked out, they
would keep locked up.

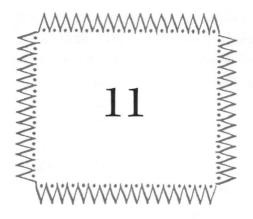

11

THE SUMMER was very dry. Even drier than predicted. May and June went fast for Black Horse. By the end of June the land was burned a deep brown and already they were hauling most of the water they needed for the stock. The wind was strong and the air often thick with blowing dust, some of it topsoil from fields that had been plowed the year before.

As he had said he would, Roger was away more all the time. By the first of July he was gone as many as four days of each week. The demands of the county job grew as the drought worsened. The job was no longer part-time.

Black Horse was the good worker Roger had hoped he would be. He was entirely dependable. He didn't have to be told what to do each day. He laid out his own work schedule from week to week and unusual was the week he didn't complete what he set out to do.

Joanne Desmet, forever the skeptic, was willing to admit only that things were going well so far, and she hoped this would continue for the season. What she was really saying was that everything was going too well and she was expecting trouble soon. Roger knew how she felt but he said nothing, and she said nothing to him about her fears.

Some ranchers around Gordon were saying this had to be the worst drought since the days of the dust bowl in the thirties. Creek beds and watering holes were completely dry. What was once mud had turned into dried chunks of earth. Farmers' corn dried out early, and other crops never even got started. The hauling of the water from as far away as Valentine so early in the year made the ranchers' cost much higher than even the most pessimistic had anticipated. But there was no alternative to hauling water, as expensive as it was. It would be unthinkable to allow the stock to die of thirst, and that was the only alternative. So haul water they did. All the time, it seemed.

Roger seldom saw Doris Mae, and this worried

him some. When he did see her it was usually from a distance, like when she was on her way to the privy. Never once had he had what he would call a real conversation. And as far as he could determine, she seldom left the house unless it was to go to the privy. God, it must be hot in there all day long, he thought, but he was trying not to think about her, except when he did see her on these rare occasions he got to wondering about the woman again. But about all he could say with much certainty was that she was a queer one.

For the first two weeks Black Horse was on the Desmet ranch he went home at lunchtime to be with Doris Mae. The first few days, she prepared lunch for him, then she stopped and started to complain all the time, telling how she missed her friends from the reservation and how they ought to make a visit home soon. Black Horse said nothing, but after a while the talk coming from Doris Mae got to bothering him so much that he began to make his own lunch in the evening and sit by the barn in the shade come lunchtime the next day. Doris Mae wasn't at all happy with this change and complained all the more bitterly in the evening when he did come home. She said he wasn't even willing to spend a half hour in the middle of the day with her, and she was right. He wasn't.

And as if he wasn't away enough during the

day, he had a habit of taking his canvas board and some paints and walking about a half mile to a dried-out creek bed where he would sit and work. He was trying to paint a scrub tree that looked like an animal, except he wasn't sure what the animal was. Sometimes he saw wildlife on his walks, but mostly he found a cool place and sat and worked until the sun went down. He was getting quite a bit of painting done.

On days when Roger was at home, sometimes the two would have lunch at the Desmet house. It was usually a working lunch, for Roger seldom had much time these days. He needed and used every moment to discuss problems around the place, and there were enough of those to talk a day and a night. At these times Black Horse took considerable care to keep from being seen by Doris Mae as he entered the Desmet house. Roger didn't notice this but Joanne did, and she wondered what it meant and what might be going on between the two Indians. She also saw Black Horse eating lunch alone down by the barn and wondered about this too, but not too much and not to the extent that she would want to invite the Indian up to lunch without Roger there. It wasn't so much she was afraid of him, although that was part of it. As it was, she knew his wife, or whatever she was, would have a fit if she found out about it. Indian women could be mighty jealous. Nobody had to tell her that. But she said nothing to Roger about what she observed. He had plenty to occupy his mind and time without thinking and worrying about the Indians. Still, she wished they weren't on the place.

Along about the middle of July there were a couple of days when Black Horse forgot a tool or needed one he didn't have and he went back to the cabin unexpectedly and found Doris Mae had been drinking. He knew right away and wondered where the liquor could have come from. Perhaps she had hid it away when they first arrived, but that didn't make good sense, for she would have drunk it all at once. There wouldn't be any left now, but there was no mistaking that she had been drinking. Later, though, around six when he got home, she was sober. She couldn't have had very much, or she would be drunk. She was no social drinker. Then, too, neither was he.

12

THE REAL TROUBLE began for Black Horse a couple of days before payday, which was about the middle of July. It had been a hard day, and after he got off from work he was having a quiet supper and Doris Mae was being unusually quiet so that he got to wondering what might be wrong. Most nights she was complaining about one thing or another. This night, however, there was no talk, so he braced himself for something to happen. He didn't have to wait long. When he got out his canvas board and some paints and said in a quiet voice that he thought he might go down to the creek bed for an hour or so to paint, she announced in a loud voice, "I am going to town myself one of these days, Elijah. You wait and see. I'm sick of this place. Sick, you hear me?"

He didn't answer her. He seldom did. When he got through fixing a paint brush he looked over at her. She was watching him, looking for his reaction. She was sober. He was sure of that.

"I will give the baby to you and have you watch him all day like I do. How would you like that, Elijah?"

Now he was folding a piece of canvas and thinking about what it would take to satisfy her. When they were back on the reservation she had complained all the time. She said she didn't like living in with his family and she wanted a place of her own. So he took her away from there and got her a good place to live and got himself a decent job and she was still complaining. Well, it was just too bad about her, because he wasn't taking her back to the reservation for a visit or to Gordon to see friends from the reservation either. He knew what would happen if they went into Gordon. They would drink. She knew this too. And above all else, Roger Desmet knew this. He knew what even one visit to Gordon, the wrong kind of visit anyway, might do to his carefully laid plans for the summer. It was just for that reason Black Horse had Desmet holding his cash for him, even doing the grocery shopping for the two of them. Roger didn't ask embarrassing questions like why. He knew what was going on. He just nodded his head that he understood and said sure, anything you want. You tell me how you want to do it. He was good that way, Roger, he'd been around Indians plenty. But Doris Mae—well, she was something else again. He couldn't explain to her satisfaction any of what he was doing or trying to do. She didn't even bother trying to understand. Whatever he said to her she wouldn't accept anyway.

Damn, he thought, even Doris Mae's going to have to learn some day to live away from the reservation. If she didn't, he wasn't going to stay with her much longer, although he couldn't quite see himself leaving either. Why? He wasn't sure why, his reason changed almost weekly—but he would stay with her. He told himself the reason was the kids. He didn't want to lose these kids like he had his others. He had got to drinking after Laurene died, he was so torn up about her death, and somebody at the Bureau of Indian Affairs came along and took his kids. Some social worker. By the time he sobered up, and that was several weeks later, he was told he had signed papers giving up his kids permanently and they were in a home near Mobridge, South Dakota. A Catholic home. And he couldn't go up to visit them. It wasn't allowed, they told him. He tried once to get in to see those two, a boy and a girl, like the two he had now. He never succeeded. He still wondered about them a lot. He knew they had to be mostly grown by this time, and he wondered if they ever thought about him. Years later he heard they were adopted, but that was all he could learn. He didn't know if it was an Indian or white family that took them, although he guessed it was by whites, which was okay, he supposed, so long as they were taken care of right. But he wouldn't ever allow that to happen again. Never!

Doris Mae kept talking at him. A constant stream of words, half of which he didn't hear.

"Elijah, you got your pictures to work every evening. I got nothing, nobody to talk to, and nothing to do all day, and you don't ever want to talk to me at night. Just sit around and paint your crummy paintings, all you ever do."

She was furious, he knew, for she got around to talking about the quality of his paintings only when she was very, very angry with him.

"We don't go anywhere on days off. Don't that ol' white man give you money enough to spend, or don't he trust you?"

She never referred to Roger by name. It was always the white man or the white woman.

"He afraid you will run off and get drunk on him? That one," she pointed toward the Desmet house, "he don't trust Indians. I can see the way he watches this place all the time. He don't think I see him looking, but I do."

Her anger and the hostility in her voice changed. She took another approach, almost pleading with him.

"Elijah, there's a lot of Indian people in Gordon from the reservation. I bet some of our friends from Corn Creek come over here sometimes." She knew they did and so did he.

And they would be more than willing to help him spend his money, he thought, getting drunk, and even coming home for a visit and stay on for a few days, move in maybe. He knew exactly what might happen if they met friends in Gordon. It had happened before and he didn't, indeed, wouldn't allow it to happen this time.

"Look, Doris Mae," he said, "Roger Desmet is okay. But he knows Indian people pretty good, much better than you understand white people. If you would talk to him sometime, Doris Mae, you might see that he is a pretty good fellow. But he knows what causes the trouble and he's got a right to worry and look after what is his. He has a lot going here and things aren't any good right now, and they ain't getting better. The same things are happening in a lot of the ranches around here. They are all having a hard time. You can see that for yourself, woman. You aren't blind."

"Bullshit, Elijah. That's just bullshit and you know it. He uses you. He pays you less than a white man, I bet. Don't he?"

She didn't wait for an answer. She didn't know what he-made because he never told her. Now he never would.

"That's why he hires you and gives you a little shack to live in. You come so cheap and he knows it."

"Little shack, is it! Why, it is a better house than you ever had in your life, and how do you say thank you? Not by keeping the place clean like a good woman would. Oh, no, not you! It is a pigpen! Look around—dirty clothes everywhere and you don't even put away the things we came here with. They are still in the boxes where you dropped them. If you did some work around here, Doris Mae, you would have less time to complain and find things wrong. And who told you lots of Indians go to Gordon? Or have you been there already?"

He was mad now and she knew it. She said nothing.

"Naw, you haven't been there. I can tell. You're too afraid to go there by yourself. You might get lost. You haven't been anywhere unless I took you. Sometimes I don't know why I stay with you, woman! I really don't! You act like an ignorant Indian! With nothing up here." He tapped the side of his head.

"If you're so damn lonesome while I am away working, why don't you go up and visit the white woman, Joanne? Because she is white don't mean she won't be friendly with you. She would like to talk with you, I bet. Maybe even have coffee with you some morning. She don't have anybody to talk to either. But I think she thinks you don't like her and you don't like white people."

That was the simple truth. He had had no conversation with Joanne Desmet, not about Doris Mae, anyway. But he was confident the woman would make Doris Mae welcome if she went up some morning.

He no sooner mentioned the white woman when he wished he hadn't.

"You interested in the white woman, Elijah? You like Joanne? Is that it? You call her Joanne, do you? Is that why you're up there all the time for? I see you go in there. You don't think I see you but I do. You're after that white woman's ass, is that it?"

He could see the suspicion in her face and anger in her eyes. She truly believed she had uncovered something important.

"You want to go to bed with her, don't you? Or maybe you have already!"

He laughed. This made her angrier, as he

knew it would. She would be more determined to find out what was going on between her man and the big white woman. She was convinced now that something was happening between them. He had something to hide and she would find out exactly what.

"Now I see it all real clear. I see why you're so friendly with the big white woman. You like what she is giving you every day. That's why you don't come home at noontime and you don't pay any attention to me at night. You go up there all the time, don't you? You're a big fool, Elijah. They don't like Indian people. Not the white man or the white woman. I bet they talk about us all the time when we're not around. I bet they say how dirty we are and like savages and we talk Indian instead of English. They laugh at us too, I am sure. Laugh at our Indian ways. Our language. But you don't care, do you, Elijah, so long as you get some of that white ass. That right, Elijah?"

Where does she get her ideas? he thought. He went back to mixing some paints. He would paint at home now. If he left, she would only get more upset. He was working on a landscape, a tourist painting of a buffalo on the plains in tall grass. Tall grass that didn't exist anymore. The land where the tall grass was once was all fenced in and being used for grazing. The buffalo were gone too, except for a few in reserves like the one near Valentine, Nebraska, and in the Black Hills. But he could sell hundreds of paintings with buffalo grazing, if the season was a good one.

"Doris Mae, you don't know *anything!* I *swear* you don't!"

He was no longer angry and his voice was low and soft. He shook his head as if to say, "I don't understand you sometimes," and of course he didn't, sometimes.

"You're such a fool! I mean, me and the white woman. Why that idea is plain silly. Crazy, even! Roger is with me anytime I am in that house. You know that. He invites me up there; for lunch, sometimes."

What he was telling her wasn't entirely the truth. One day he was supposed to meet Roger for lunch and Roger was held up and couldn't get home, but Black Horse was there and a nervous Joanne Desmet served him lunch. There were only the two of them in the house and Black Horse left as quickly as he could to keep the woman from feeling too uncomfortable there alone with him. What she was afraid of he didn't know. The talk, maybe. Something more, even. He didn't know and didn't much care. He wouldn't tell Doris Mae any of this, however.

"You eat lunch up there, do you, Elijah?" She

said she saw him go in there many a day. What did she think he did up there when he was going in at lunchtime? "So what is wrong with my lunch?"

"Nothing. Nothing at all, Doris Mae. The food is good except you don't ever put anything out for me. I sure wish you wouldn't keep acting like the jealous, ignorant Indian. I wish you wouldn't. I swear, sometimes...."

"And act like your important white friends? Is that how you would have me act, Elijah? Like your new white friends, huh? Never!"

She spat in the corner near his paint supplies.

"You better be careful what you go around saying about me and the white woman, Doris Mae. I am warning you."

The anger was returning. She was getting to him. She had a way of doing this.

"You hear me good." Now he was lecturing her. She knew he wasn't joking. She looked away rather than meet his steady glare.

"You can cause a lot of trouble around here with that kind of talk. And I will fix you good if you do that. I promise you I will!"

She watched his anger build. It was the way she liked to see him get when he was drunk, because then he became crazy-acting and unpredictable, and she didn't know what he would do next. When he was sober, however, she was more afraid of him when he became angry, although she liked the attention he was paying her. None of this would she have admitted, not even to herself. But in truth, Doris Mae got nervous when Black Horse was sober for a long stretch. Now he hadn't had a drink since they left the reservation, and that had been almost three months. She was also discovering that he acted quite different when he was without alcohol for long periods of time. He was almost strange to her and very distant and she hated to say it, but he acted more like the white people all the time. She understood him much better, preferred him, when he was drinking. Then they laughed and ran around to all sorts of good places and had fun together. Working on a ranch in Gordon wasn't any kind of life. What did it get him or her? A little money maybe, but not that much. And it was so dull and routine. She missed her friends and family and the parties they had. Now it got so he would lecture her more all the time, like the white schoolteachers did on the reservation when she was a girl. Like them, he would be telling her about how to get along in the white man's world. Well, damn it, she didn't care anything about that world. She missed the old Elijah who came with her to Gordon from the reservation. He was much more fun than this new man.

13

Two afternoons later, Doris Mae caught a ride into Gordon. She didn't have much money—two single-dollar bills was all—but she could find a friendly Indian or even a cowboy to buy her drinks when her money ran out. She had before, plenty of times. And if she was lucky and met somebody real friendly, maybe she would have enough money to bring back something for Elijah. Then he wouldn't be so angry with her for running off without telling him. He just might like to have a little drink with her, and that snoopy Desmet didn't need to know anything about it. They would have a quiet little party, get drunk, and that would be it. Nobody would have to know anything.

The one Indian bar in Gordon is called the Silver Spur, and while there is no sign on the outside and Doris Mae had never been there before, she had no trouble finding the place. The bar sits in the middle of the business district of Gordon with a variety store on one side and a secondhand junk shop on the other. The bar looks like it might have been an afterthought, for it was squeezed in between the other businesses.

The entrance to the bar is narrow—a green door with paint peeling. No window in front. It could have been a pool hall or the police station or a barbershop. Inside, however, the space widens and there is a room long and narrow that extends far back beyond where she could see. In the back, almost in darkness, a latticework partition separates one section of the room from the other. She guessed there was a dance floor behind the latticework. To the left of the door was a long mahogany-stained bar and in the center of the floor tables and chairs. The place was much bigger than it looked from the outside.

Doris Mae was carrying the baby Robert and had Denise by the hand when she entered the Silver Spur. She placed the baby on a table near the door and began to fumble with her wallet, trying to get out her two one-dollar bills. Nobody noticed her enter. The place was almost empty, it then being about two o'clock in the afternoon. The Silver Spur didn't come alive until after seven. Then it became truly an Indian bar in that white people who used the place in the day moved on well before seven, when reservation Indians began to arrive. The place got much too wild at night for local folks. Besides, there was another bar in the town that was off limits to Indians, or at least the Indians stayed out of there most of the time. An Indian dressed in a suit and tie and thought to be an important person from the reservation, like the tribal president, might get served in the Stockman Bar (that was the name of the place), but other Indians were told to stay out and away, and they did most of the time.

The barman was a short stocky man with a red face, with broken veins on his nose—an alcoholic's face, really. He studied her for a minute and then turned back to a conversation with a white man standing at the bar. The bartender was a half-owner in the place with another man by the name of Ramon. Ramon worked nights this week.

"I wonder what she wants," the bartender said to the cowboy. He grinned.

"Aimin' to rest some and get out of the sun, you reckon?" the cowboy said.

"Shit, they drag their kids everywhere, don't they?" the barkeep said. He looked over at Doris Mae, wondering if he knew her. She didn't look like anyone he had seen in the place, but so many Indians came and went that he couldn't be sure. Besides, a lot of them looked alike to him.

The only sound was music from the jukebox behind the latticework partition. A low, sad-sounding country-western ballad was playing, with the word 'persuaded' said over and over again.

In a short while the barkeep came over to the table where Doris Mae sat patiently. She made no demands. She knew the barman had seen her. She waited. She knew he would be around.

"A double whiskey," she told him, but he waited by the table until she showed him her money. That was another custom in Gordon. The barkeep seldom brought a round of drinks to an Indian without first seeing money. She produced the two new single-dollar bills.

After she showed him the money he was off and back again immediately with the double shot of bar whiskey. He didn't have to ask an Indian like this one if there was a particular brand she preferred. He knew she would drink any rot-gut liquor he brought.

Doris Mae stayed in that bar, drinking until after ten P.M. She left only once to go out and buy several candy bars for Denise in the variety store next door. And when the baby got hungry she breast-fed him as she sat talking to the various Indian men who came to her table to talk to her and buy her drinks. After a while there were only two men left, one a big man with a coarse face. His name was Little Bald Eagle. She knew him from the reservation, although he didn't live in Corn Creek. He said he knew Elijah.

That evening Black Horse got home from work and discovered Doris Mae had left. He thought immediately that she had returned to the reservation and for a brief moment he was both elated and depressed. In a way it is better this way, he thought. He could meet her later in the summer after his work for Desmet was done. As things were going now, she wasn't much of a help. But being alone wasn't what he wanted either. As he sat down to his paints he noticed that nothing was missing. Her clothes were there, as were the things belonging to the children. She wouldn't go off without taking these things.

That meant she's gone to Gordon, he thought, anger growing in him. And she would come home drunk no doubt, but there was nothing he could do but wait. So he painted and waited. Well after eleven—closer to twelve, really—he heard the car drive in and voices and then the car drive off. He was about to get up and go to the door when he heard the angry voice of Doris Mae speaking in Indian to Denise.

"Come on," she said roughly in a drunken tone.

He looked up from his work as she entered, pretending he hadn't heard her. She carried the baby in a soiled blanket that looked as if it might have been dragged on the floor, it was so dirty. She stumbled and almost fell through the doorway and he got up and took the baby from her, carrying him into the bedroom and putting him on the bed. He stank of shit and he very much needed a diaper change, which Black Horse decided he would do in a minute. Next he picked up Denise—she was practically asleep on her feet—and carried her to the bedroom. She was asleep before he laid her down. The kid was exhausted.

Doris Mae was drunker than he had seen her in a long time. She carried a paper bag that he guessed contained a bottle. She weaved around the room as if she didn't know where she was or was going and when he came near her she pulled away and grinned. "Stay away, you can't have my bottle, Elijah." she said. "My friend Little Bald Eagle bought it for me. How come you're home, Elijah? Why aren't you up in the big house visiting with your new white friends? I know you're not there because her husband is home and he don't like you fucking his woman when he's around. Is that the reason, Elijah?"

When she was drunk she literally spat out his name like bad food.

The bag she held contained a quart of gin. She placed it on his paint table where he could see it good. She knew he liked gin more than anything else.

"Did you have to drag the little ones all around Gordon?" he asked.

"You want me to leave them with you, I suppose?"

She knew if she went to him and said she was leaving for Gordon, he would have tried to stop her.

"What do you care what I do anyway, Elijah?" She was slurring her words and weaving dangerously as if she might fall. He paid no attention to her or tried not to, anyway.

"What do you care what I do?" she said again. "You're so busy with your new white friends you shouldn't worry about what Doris Mae is doing. She's just having fun for herself." She said this with a big laugh.

"But I had a good time, a real good time. The best time I've had since I came to this place. Where is this place anyway?" She said this with another laugh, less loud. "I've forgotten where we are.

"Nowhere, that's where. Now I remember. We are nowhere and you like it that way, Elijah. I don't know what kind of man you are or what kind of woman you think I am, keeping us way out here and with Gordon so close."

He told her to quiet down, fearing Desmet would hear and come down to find out what was the problem.

"Oh," she said in a whisper, "you afraid your white friends will see me like this and won't approve." She laughed again, this time louder than before, much louder.

Desmet is sure to hear, Black Horse thought, beginning to get angry with her.

"Well, let me tell you, fuck them. I don't care if they like me or not. They are not my friends. They're your friends." And with that she turned and extended her middle finger toward Desmet's house. She almost fell down trying to do this and Black Horse laughed out loud. She could be funny when she was drunk.

She made her way, after considerable struggle, to the table where the bottle of gin sat in the paper bag.

She poured herself a drink and one for him and sat down.

"I met some good people from St. Francis. Real friendly people who bought me drinks all night. They even gave me the money for this bottle for you. I bought this for you, Elijah. I shouldn't have, but I did."

He looked at the bottle of gin from which she had poured the two large drinks.

"You know one of the fellows I met? Little Bald Eagle. He says he knows you."

Black Horse knew him, all right. He had once almost got in a fight with Lloyd Little Bald Eagle. He didn't like him. What's more, he didn't trust him. A rumor had it that Little Bald Eagle once stuck a knife in the back of another Indian who was foolish enough to have turned his back on him after an argument in a bar. The man survived, but barely. He was hospitalized for a long, long time.

"He's a real nice fellow. Knows how to treat a lady." She said this in a way that suggested he did more than buy her drinks and that was why he knew how to treat a lady. Black Horse noticed, but he didn't answer right away. He thought some about what she said and then said, "You're lucky you got home safely. Little Bald Eagle is a bum." He thought of telling her the story of the knifing but decided not to bother.

"You should stay away from a character like Little Bald Eagle. He's no good."

"He's real nice, Elijah. What you heard is only talk. Ugly talk. He is a real gentleman." She picked up the glass she had poured for Black Horse and handed it to him. He took it but drank none. He just looked at it for a moment as if trying to make up his mind, then he sipped it as if to determine it was really good gin and then, with a quick gulp, he downed the liquor, which had to be more than two shots in a water glass. It was not mixed with anything. He never drank gin with a mixer except a beer chaser and only sometimes did he have the chaser. He quickly followed the first glass with another and then still another, and by this time he was so dizzy he had to hold himself up by leaning onto his paint table.

When he spoke his words sounded far away like outside his body, but soon he began to feel good and in control of the situation, although he knew he wasn't.

Laughter punctuated his conversation and he didn't make much sense. Doris Mae observed the change immediately and laughed along with him.

She watched him getting drunk, not gradual like she had, but fast. But she knew him best when he was like this and this was the way she liked him some of the time. Life was more normal this way.

As he got drunker he was having trouble even standing and he wanted to go outside for air, but he thought of Desmet, who might be watching from his house. A few minutes passed and more drinks and he no longer cared if Desmet saw him. He could always get another job. Hadn't he done a good job for Roger? And weren't all the ranchers in the area hungry for good dependable help like him? Hell, Desmet shouldn't stand in the way of a little fun for one night. It didn't hurt anything.

Soon he began to focus on what Doris Mae was saying. He had heard her say something about him not being much of a provider when he was living on the ranch of another man who happened to be a white man. He ought to be able to make it on his own, she said, have his own place. Same old shit that she was saying again. What was different was that she was now saying it wasn't natural for an Indian to be living the life of a white man on a white man's land with no family or friends around. This part annoyed him, although he knew it too was a bunch of horseshit. She never stops complaining, he thought angrily. Nothing was ever good enough for her, damn her.

"You're not a rancher, you're just a hired hand like a slave, Elijah. Like some nigger. Hired for less money than a white man would get, even less than they would pay a nigger. The white guy, he makes the money and you do all the work. Why, he isn't even around here most of the time. You're a

108

regular sucker, that's what you are, Elijah. You get next to nothing. You get the shit, the leftovers. All you get out of this is a chance to talk to the white woman. Maybe fuck her sometimes when her husband is away, huh, Elijah?"

She came up close to his face and was nearly shouting at him. He felt like hitting her.

"You like her, don't you, Elijah? I can tell. And she wants to go to bed with you, don't she, Elijah? Tell me the truth."

He could barely hold up his head and her talk wasn't clear now, but the hum of her voice was aggravating. All he kept hearing was his name Elijah. "Isn't it, Elijah?" she kept saying. Isn't what?

She kept talking at him. "You go ahead and try something funny with her, Elijah, and she will scream rape. She will say the filthy savage of an Indian who works for less pay than niggers tried to rape her. That's you, Elijah. Then you will see what she thinks of Indians and you'll come back to your people real fast and you won't think of becoming a white man after that."

Deep down that's what worried her. That he would become in his actions more white than Indian and she wouldn't know how to act around him, much less live with him.

She was screaming now, "You listen to me good, Elijah. You go after that woman and she will

109

call her husband to beat you up. He would kill you, he would be so angry that a dirty Indian touched his pure white wife. You may be a good worker for him, a good slave, but you're still a dirty reservation Indian. Don't forget that, Elijah. Don't you ever forget it. That's all you are to them. You're not much above human."

He looked up at her now and she moved away. His head was clearing and he was hearing what she said.

"Shut up, Doris Mae. Shut the fuck up," he said. "I don't want to hear your voice anymore."

Then he grinned as he thought of something to say to her—to get back at what she had been saying.

"How do you know the white woman don't want me herself? How do you know she didn't come to me and ask for it? Her husband is busy and away a lot. She might be lonesome. How do you know, Doris Mae?"

He laughed as he looked at her face. She didn't know.

She listened to him without once interrupting him.

"And how do you know I haven't been with her before now? I had lots of chances, more than you know. Lots of time alone in that big house up there." He pointed in the direction of the house.

"You don't know if I ever touched her, do you, Doris Mae? I may have laid my head between those big soft breasts."

He laughed, he was enjoying this.

But she was taking him very seriously.

"You don't know, do you?" he said, taunting her more. "There are lots of things you don't know, Doris Mae, because you're an ignorant reservation Indian with no education who doesn't know shit. Why, you don't even know how to live around white people." He laughed again.

He knew her reaction would be swift and angry. She cared not at all that he called her an ignorant reservation Indian. He had called her that more times than she could remember. But the part about the white woman was new and she believed what he said.

"You been with that woman, Elijah?" She was screaming now, and the louder her voice went, the more he laughed.

She staggered over to where he was standing but he pushed her away hard and she almost fell, but she came back again.

"I will kill you if you have. I swear I will. And I will cut her throat in her sleep."

He laughed again. He had her believing him and that was pleasant. He knew she wouldn't kill anyone—she wasn't capable of such a thing—but

111

if she met up with Joanne Desmet she might start a fight, a knock-down roll-in-the-dust kind of fight. Not a fight with words.

"I will beat the hell out of her, Elijah. I warn you I will do it. I will go right over there now and get her out of bed and fight with her in the front yard and with her husband there. I don't care."

That would be something funny to witness, he thought with another loud laugh. She was crazy enough to try something like that, but he wouldn't let her do it and she knew that.

She started toward the door as if she might be serious in going up to the Desmet place but she tripped over a cardboard box and fell on the floor. This brought another howl of laughter from Black Horse while she lay on the floor cursing him.

"You can hardly stand up, Doris Mae, how you going to fight the big white woman with the soft breasts? You know, I've never seen such nice soft breasts in my life. I swear. She has the best I've ever touched."

He used his hands to show her how big and round and full they were.

She struggled to her feet and started for the door again but the change in his voice stopped her. He sounded almost sober to her now and very earnest.

"Don't you go anywhere," he warned.

Then he walked over to her, held both her hands as she struggled to get free, and said, "You go over there and get those people out of bed and I will beat the hell out of you." Then, as if to show that he meant what he said, he slapped her hard across the face until she began to cry, then he pushed her in the corner with the paper bags and cardboard boxes. He went back to the gin bottle on the paint table.

She was frightened, but in a peculiar way excited. When he was like this it was exciting. He didn't know what he was doing and she didn't know what next to expect from him.

The most frightened she had ever been around him was two years before when he discovered her on the outhouse floor with no clothes on and one of the young Running Bear boys trying to mount her. He was so mad that time he tore a board from the door of the outhouse, forgetting about Running Bear, who quietly left, and began to beat the hell out of her with that board. It was the worst beating she ever got from him. She never forgot.

But now it was her time to do some tormenting.

"You think you're the only one who can find somebody to be with, Elijah? That's what you think?"

Now it was his turn to listen. He waited and

watched her. She stood in the corner among the boxes and bags.

"I was with a white guy today. A rancher who lives outside of Valentine."

She was making this up but she made it sound convincing, or at least she thought she had until Black Horse began to laugh.

She went on just the same. "He bought me drinks and he was good to me. Treated me like a lady."

"Who are you trying to fool?" he said. "No rancher would have you, Doris. None of them would fool around with you. They would be too embarrassed. Their friends would make fun of them, laugh at them for not being able to tell the difference between a good-looking woman and a hag like you."

She started to cry but he didn't stop.

"Those cowboys didn't want sick-looking skinny worn-out Indian women. They want young girls seventeen or eighteen who are just starting out."

He was right. She said no more about the white rancher. When she spoke again the story was more believable.

"Little Bald Eagle thought I was pretty good though." She smiled, showing spaces where teeth had once been.

"We done it in the car," she said, and they had. Little Bald Eagle had never in his life bought any Indian woman several drinks without getting something in return. Had she refused him, he would have beat her senseless. She knew this when she accepted the drinks, and what's more, so did Black Horse.

"That weasel would screw a snake if somebody would hold its head," Black Horse said. He believed her story. It was hardly a first time for her. Some of her worst beatings came after he found out about her being with another man.

"So you was with him, was you?" He was very angry now and she was frightened.

"Damn you, Doris Mae. You sure are hard up. He is no better than a common murderer. Kills Indian people, he does, and you mess around with him. You let him do it to you? You didn't try to resist him?"

"I tried to stop him, Elijah," she lied. She was alarmed at what he might do. He was capable of about anything when he was this drunk.

She began to cry again.

"I didn't want to do it but he would have beat me up. You know how big he is. You know what he is like, Elijah. I am telling you the truth, honest."

There was an obvious pleading in her voice for understanding. He didn't know whether she was

115

telling the truth. He tried to look at her face but she quickly looked away and began to cry again.

What happened next was what she most feared.

"Well, Doris Mae, we will take a little ride into Gordon and see what Little Bald Eagle has to say about all this you tell me. And if you're lying, Doris Mae, I will beat the hell out of you and if he done what you said—if he forced you to do it—I'm going to kill him."

"Please, not now, Elijah," she begged him. "It is too late. The bars will be closed by the time we get there. And how will we go? We don't have a car. Besides, he isn't there now. He left." She didn't know this but she thought there was a good possibility that he had returned to the reservation after he brought her home. But she would have told Black Horse anything to keep him home.

"I bet he's gone to Crockston," she said. "I bet that is where he is. Let's not go, Elijah, please."

She was not just frightened for herself, for if Little Bald Eagle was still in the Gordon bar he might kill Black Horse if a fight started. She knew Little Bald Eagle well enough to know he could drink for hours and still be quite sober. He would be no man to pick a fight with under the best of circumstances, considering his size and reputation as a fighter. Drunk, a man might have no chance at all against him.

But Black Horse didn't believe her nor did he believe Little Bald Eagle had left the Silver Spur. He was ready to leave for Gordon, and when she protested again he slapped her across the face and dragged her out of the house, pulling her behind him like he was leading a child. She was sobbing softly.

They passed in full view of the Desmet house but Black Horse didn't think anything more this night about Roger Desmet. His mind was not on ranch work.

Out on the state highway a carload of young Indians cruising and drinking cheap whiskey picked them up. Black Horse didn't notice, and wouldn't have cared if he had, but the young Indians were heavily armed with shotguns and rifles and even handguns. What they were looking for they didn't say. They were friendly enough to him and Doris Mae and generously passed their large bottle of whiskey to both of them. Each took ample swallows. They left the couple about a half mile from the center of Gordon, explaining how they didn't wish, for what should have been obvious reasons, to drive into the business district of Gordon. So Black Horse and Doris Mae hiked the rest of the way into town.

14

DESMET SAT IN HIS front room with the light out,
thinking. He was depressed and very tired. He had
witnessed it all, had seen everything there was to
see, and had heard even more when he went out
and stood near the corral not far from the little
house. He didn't understand the Indian language
but he did know a quarrel when he heard one.

And he knew what it meant or could mean to
his plans. It would be by only the most unusual
kind of good fortune that after this binge Black
Horse could be kept working. He doubted if he
would have that kind of luck.

"I should have turned them away when I saw that woman, goddamnit!" he mumbled. "I should have seen it coming." He knew she was trouble and had ignored the signs, damn fool that he was.

The man was doing so well too, and now this, and with the drought even worse than predicted. The ranch simply couldn't be left unattended even if that meant leaving his county job, which he could not afford to do. What choice did he have though?

He looked at his wristwatch. It was after midnight. The bars would be closing and that would mean Black Horse and Doris Mae should return soon, if they were coming back at all. There were no guarantees; this might be the beginning of a several-day drunk. He would have to go over and look in on the children, who were alone. Poor creatures. What a life they lived.

They mustn't be left by themselves. He didn't want the oldest waking up and calling out for her mother or father and having no one there. It would be enough of a shock to discover him there, but at least they wouldn't be so frightened if he were there when they woke.

The house was a mess—he expected it might be, but nothing like it was. It was the first time he had been inside since the Indians had moved in. He was sure it hadn't been picked up or cleaned

119

since they arrived. Things had been moved around a bit, but that was about it.

A shame, he thought, a rotten shame. He had worked so hard on that house.

The children were still asleep when he arrived. It was then nearly one A.M. He didn't think Black Horse and Doris Mae were going to return. He sat and waited, smoking a cigarette in the dark. He sat there all night, falling asleep for a couple of hours, if for that long. With morning he looked in on the children, who still slept without a sound. Then he went up to his house, where he found his wife preparing breakfast. He poured some hot coffee and sat at the kitchen table, watching her.

She could see by his face that there was trouble with the Indians.

"I heard the commotion. Are they drinking, Roger?"

"I guess so," he said with no emotion. He was beyond being angry. He felt like a fool for having them on his place. Now it would be hard to get rid of them, if that was what it was to come to. He feared it might.

"They're not here?"

"Nope."

"What about the kids? They take them? They moved off the place, have they?"

She knew how much he needed the help Black

Horse provided, but a side of her would have been happy to know the Indians had moved out and back to the reservation where they belonged as far as she was concerned.

"They left them."

"They what? Where did they go? Are they coming back? My God, left them! Up and leave your children in the middle of the night without saying a word to anyone! I never heard of such a thing."

"You have now, for that's what they did."

"You mean those children are down there all by themselves?"

"Don't fret, Joanne. I just left them. They're okay. They're still asleep. I was there all night. Since 'bout half an hour after they staggered out of here. That must have been some before midnight. I don't know for certain."

"You got no sleep, I suppose?"

"I slept some."

The goddamn Indians made her furious. She could see how worried her husband was, and tired, dogged tired.

This will be the last time we will depend on an Indian for anything, she thought with bitterness. Never again, if she had anything to say about it, and she would for sure.

"You would think they cared more about their

kids. I mean, what if there had been a fire? If one of 'em had left a cigarette burning, there could have been a fire, heaven forbid!"

It was too horrible for Desmet to imagine. He tried not to think about it but his thoughts wandered to a news story he had read that past winter about a reservation family in St. Francis who left a six-week-old infant alone and were off drinking. There had been a fire and the baby was burned to death. He remembered throwing away that newspaper so Joanne didn't see it.

"I don't think Black Horse would go off and leave those kids alone if he was sober," Roger said wearily. "But nothing that woman does surprises me. I think Black Horse is more responsible."

"Responsible! You can't make excuses for him, Roger. It is the same thing. He left the kids alone. There is no excuse for that. Being drunk isn't good enough for me."

"Indians are different when they get to drinking," Roger said. "I swear it affects them in a different way from white people. It is something in them. The way they're made, I guess. That's why I tried so hard to keep that bastard sober. I knew what he would do if I didn't." He seldom cursed, but now even curse words seemed mild and not enough.

15

WHEN BLACK HORSE entered the Silver Spur he was nearly falling-down drunk. The barkeep immediately picked up the phone and called the sheriff's office. Black Horse announced to the mostly empty barroom that he'd come for Little Bald Eagle and he was going to kill him. The barman reached under the bar and cocked his shotgun. He hoped he wouldn't have to use it, but he would if he had to.

Fortunately, Little Bald Eagle wasn't there and hadn't been there for a couple of hours, but that didn't keep Black Horse from hollering and making threats and frightening several of the patrons so that they moved away from the door where he stood waving his arms like a madman. One man got up and left.

In less than five minutes two large white men appeared at the door behind Black Horse and, following them was a smaller man, although by no means small. The smaller man was the sheriff, Abe Pates. The other two were his deputies.

The two deputies came up behind Black Horse and, one on each side, grabbed him by his arms. He resisted, but they pinned his arms behind him, although they didn't use handcuffs. He couldn't move.

Sheriff Pates then walked up to Black Horse and said, "Look, fella, quiet down. You're not doin' any killin' round here, hear me?" He prodded Black Horse with a night stick.

Black Horse apparently didn't hear; he ignored the sheriff and kept talking and struggling against the men who held him. The sheriff studied Black Horse for a long time as if trying to make a decision and then he lifted his club and hit him hard aside of the neck and then again below the knees and once more at about the level of the kidneys. There was no more talk or struggle. The two deputies dragged a limp Black Horse to the waiting police car.

The sheriff nodded in the direction of the bar-keep, whose name was Eddie. Eddie smiled approval and waved. Doris Mae sat at the corner table and watched all of this. She was grateful Little Bald Eagle wasn't there, for Black Horse might be dead now instead of beat up and in jail. That night she slept in the alley waiting for Black Horse to be released from jail the next morning.

16

WHEN BY MIDDAY Black Horse and Doris Mae had not returned to Desmet's place, Roger Desmet called the sheriff.

Yep, they had him.

Nope, he wouldn't be released right away. He had caused quite a disturbance the night before.

No, he hadn't hurt anybody or done any damage but he was very wild and they wanted him in jail as a precaution. They wanted him very sober when he left, and that might take a while yet.

All of this Roger had from a deputy.

"If you want this Indian, Roger, come around

later and see Abe. If it was me, though, I wouldn't want him back."

Roger promised he would do that and along about three P.M. he drove to Gordon to see Sheriff Pates.

The Gordon jail is located along a back alley in a warehouse that once had been used as a feed storage building. Now it was a modern jail. The state and federal governments had jointly put up the money to build an up-to-date facility. The sheriff liked to boast that he could comfortably keep thirty prisoners in his jail without being overcrowded.

"We've got your crazy Indian," Sheriff Pates greeted Roger as he walked through the door.

"And he is a crazy one, though he ain't ever been arrested over here so we don't have a folder on him. He didn't volunteer much information. I guess he thought he might get out without you hearin' about his trouble. Damn fool to think that, ain't he? Nuthin' goes on that ain't talked about in this town. I heard you had one of them working out at your place, Roger, so I was going to call you if we couldn't figure out who this character was."

Desmet sat on the corner of the sheriff's desk and looked over his shoulder at the file they now had for Black Horse. There was only one sheet of paper in it.

"Your boy is kind of embarrassed about how he acted last night. You ought to be careful around a fellow like that, Roger. When he's been drinking. He was awful ugly and he's strong. Why, when we got him back here we had to fight with him to get him in the cell. 'Course I had to use my stick on him some to teach him who was boss."

Desmet guessed what that meant. "He's all right, Abe?" he asked.

In spite of all that had happened, Desmet still felt a responsibility for having Black Horse on his place. He didn't want to see the man injured, even if it was something he brought on himself, which clearly it was as far as he was concerned.

"Oh, he's mostly all right. A little sore maybe, but he brought it on hisself," the sheriff said. "Indians have hard heads."

"What are you going to do with him?" Desmet asked. "You holding him on any charges?"

"I ought to be, but I am not. He didn't break up nuthin' except my poker game and I was losin' so I don't suppose I can fault him for that. If you want him back, Roger, I will give him to you, but promise me you keep him out of Gordon. Keep him on your place.

"I can't make that kind of promise, Abe. Shit, he ain't my kid or something. I don't want him in here in town any more than you do, but I can't tell him where to go or what to do when he's not working. You know that."

"Okay, okay. But first I want to talk to him and make it real clear to him that I don't want him around here causing no more trouble."

You do that. Tell him to fly straight, not that it is likely to do you much good, Desmet thought. But tell him anyway. Maybe he will listen this time. Tough job being sheriff. He wouldn't want it for any pay and he knew the job didn't pay much.

Roger let out a low whistle when he saw Black Horse after Sheriff Pates finished lecturing him in the cell where Roger couldn't see or hear.

What a mess he was! One eye was closed and his face was black and blue everywhere. They had beat hell out of him, that was plain to see. Was it necessary? Roger wanted to ask. Was he resisting that much? But he didn't ask. It was enough that he was there getting an Indian out of jail. That act alone was enough to get a man labeled as an Indian liker, if not lover. But then too, almost every rancher had hired Indian help one time or another and they knew how important it was to keep the man working, especially in a hard year.

Black Horse walked with a limp, but otherwise he seemed okay and he didn't complain about his treatment.

The first thing he asked about was his kids.

Are they okay? He wanted to know. And next he asked about the work he had missed and began promising that he would make up the time and that the next day he would be on the job again. Desmet was skeptical, if only because he knew the man was going to need at least two or three days to recover from his injuries. He didn't say anything, however. They didn't talk much on the ride back to the ranch.

Joanne was at the gate when they drove in. She came out to meet them, which told Desmet there must be yet more trouble.

Now what?

"Roger, you wouldn't believe the language that woman uses." She didn't care that Black Horse was with him. She ignored him and looked straight at her husband. Black Horse hobbled off toward the house in back.

"I thought she was going to hit me. I swear I thought she would. She's been drinking. It is terrible what is going on. She accused me of sleeping with him."

She spoke barely above a whisper as she told Roger what Doris Mae had said to her. It was as if there might be somebody listening to retell the story.

"Can you imagine such a thing for her to say?

"It is so embarrassing. Me with that Indian. If

130

it ever got out. You know how stories are. I would die, Roger. Just die. People can be so cruel and want to believe anything, especially if it is juicy and involves sex. The gossip would be awful. My God, Roger, you don't suppose she has been saying these things in the bars? Connecting my name with her husband?"

"Oh, I don't think so, Joanne," he said, but he wasn't very sure or, he supposed, very convincing, and she knew he had no idea what Doris Mae said in the bars, and he didn't. She could have said about anything.

"She was angry and drunk and probably said it off the top of her head," he said. "I wouldn't think much about it. It will only make you that much more upset."

He put his arm around her and walked her up to the house. She began to cry as they reached it. He was exhausted.

He knew right then the Indians would have to go. What Black Horse said about resting and going back to work wouldn't be possible now. Too much had happened. He would have to figure how to get them off the place without a fuss.

Desmet sat in the kitchen, sipping coffee and thinking about how to give Black Horse the news to pack up and leave, when there was a scream from a woman in back. It had to be Doris Mae.

Then another scream and swearing and he ran toward the house to see Black Horse staggering away toward the highway, carrying a near-empty bottle of gin. They passed without speaking.

When he reached the house he found Doris Mae with a cloth over her nose, trying to stop a nosebleed. Her nose was spread across her face like it might be broken and she had what would certainly turn into a black eye and a cut on her head.

She screamed at him when he entered. She was very drunk.

"See the trouble I get 'cause of you, white man." He thought she was going to spit at him.

"See what Elijah do to me 'cause of you?"

"Me," he almost laughed in her face but he was too angry. "What you talking about, woman? What the hell do I have to do with what goes on between you and your crazy husband?"

"You brung Elijah here where he don't belong. That is bad. He's an Indian, no rancher, and he ain't ought to live with white people doing white man's work. He should be on the reservation with his family and friends, where people want him and understand him good."

My God, so it is my fault now, Desmet thought bitterly. That's a come-around if I ever heard one.

Then he exploded at Doris Mae.

"I didn't make you or him come over here and I regret the day I decided to have you. If I knew the trouble you people would be I wouldn't have let you within a mile of the place. Goddamn you. Now, pick up your things and get the hell out of here. I will take you to the reservation in an hour. If you're not ready you can walk home. I don't care. And I am not taking you clear out to Corn Creek. I won't drive that far. I will drop you at St. Francis. I will go no further. Now get packed up, goddamn it!"

Doris Mae didn't answer him. She began to pack their stuff and he went home, and as he had said he would, he took her to St. Francis, South Dakota, and dropped her there. She had relatives in nearby Spring Creek and went there for the night. The next day she caught a ride out to Corn Creek.

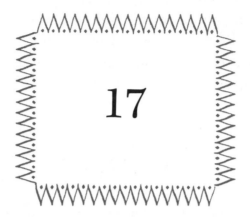

17

JIM BENNION opened the door to his room one morning and was about to throw out a pan of soapy water that had sat overnight in his sink when he saw Doris Mae standing there. He nearly let fly at her with the water. He hadn't been looking for any-one to be standing on his step. He didn't hear her knocking. He gasped when he saw her face, almost dropping the water on his own feet.

"My God, what the hell happened to you? You been in a car wreck?" That was all he could think of at the moment. He poured the water out next to his steps.

"Elijah beat me up," she said matter-of-factly.

Her left eye was closed, her nose had to be broken, and there were cuts up into her scalp and a knot the size of a golf ball aside her head. He felt like asking her if Black Horse had used a baseball bat, but he didn't.

She spoke with difficulty because her lips were puffy, actually purple colored, and she talked out of the side of her mouth. Apparently that was easier.

Bennion didn't ask for the particulars. They were getting to be all too familiar for him.

"Well, come in," he said at last. He was annoyed and he wasn't sure why. She hadn't done or said anything out of the way. Not yet. He knew, though, that her condition meant Black Horse was in jail or in trouble in some way or else she wouldn't be on his doorstep. She wanted something. That was obvious, but what it was wasn't so obvious.

I am not up for this, he thought. Not this morning with a new elder coming. Why me? Why today?

"Where is Black Horse now?" he asked, expecting to hear the usual reply, in jail.

"I don't know," she said. "Maybe dead. I don't know, Jim Bennion." She started to cry, but stopped almost as soon as she began.

"You got to help him come home," she announced. "He's actin' crazy-like and drinking too much. I know him real good. He don't belong there with them white people. He belongs here in Corn Creek on the reservation. With his own kind."

Then she said, "I think he took up with the white woman."

"Desmet's wife?"

She nodded her head.

Bennion was genuinely astonished. He didn't believe she could be serious. But he could tell she meant what she said, incredible as it sounded to him. Black Horse knew better than that—not that Bennion could actually picture the wife of a white rancher like Desmet tangling with an Indian who, among other things, was a pretty bad alcoholic. It didn't make good sense. Still, one could never be sure about such things. Stranger things than this could happen, did all the time.

Now it was clear what she wanted of him. He was to go to Gordon and get Black Horse to come home to Doris Mae so she wouldn't be too lonesome.

In a way Black Horse might be better off where he was, he thought. He was away from Doris Mae and that didn't have to be bad for a short while. She did nothing to encourage Black Horse to stop drinking. Maybe he would now sober up and go back to work for Desmet and everything would be okay again. But he knew deep down that that wasn't going to happen. Usually once Black Horse started drinking he didn't stop until he was being carried off to jail. That had been the pattern in the past.

Bennion had considered visiting with Black Horse and Doris Mae toward the end of the summer, if only to see how things were going. Well, already he could see how things were going. Not well. There was no need for him to go to Gordon to see that for himself but he knew he would go in case he could be of help in some small way. He knew if Black Horse got arrested in Nebraska he might stay there for a while. Things weren't the same there as on the reservation, and with the tensions running high between whites and Indians in the Gordon area a man might get himself killed easily over there simply by having too much to say. When Black Horse was drunk, that was exactly his problem. He had much too much to say and often said it to the wrong people.

"I will go, Doris Mae, but I am not making any promises. I can't promise I will bring him back. No way. I will drive to Gordon, see if I can find him, and that's all I can promise. It will be up to him if he wants to ride back with me. I won't try to convince him to come home."

"He listens to you good and likes you," she said.

Here comes the flattery, Bennion thought. The bit about how Indian people liked him and trusted him and the rest. He had heard it a few times from different persons, when they wanted something from him.

"He says good things about you, Jim Bennion. Says how you are fair with Indian people. They trust what you say and..."

"Okay, I am going, Doris Mae, but remember what I said. I am not promising to bring him home." He meant it too, but he was flattered, as he always was, when an Indian—any Indian, even Doris Mae—said he was fair and thought well of by the people.

She heard the part she wanted to hear, he thought, as she left. She wanted to hear him say he would go to Gordon, because if he said he would go she knew he would. She didn't hear the part he said about maybe not bringing home Black Horse. Oh, she heard it all right, but she tuned him out when he said it.

Bennion didn't have time to remind Doris Mae that Black Horse had a deal, a commitment, with the white rancher, Desmet, and he shouldn't just up and leave in the middle of the season. He should have told her he might encourage Black Horse to stay and honor his promise to Desmet. He didn't say any of this, though, and he supposed it was as well that he hadn't.

18

THE NEXT DAY he drove the seventy-five miles to
Gordon. His plan was simple. He would go right to
the Desmet ranch to see if Black Horse might have
returned, and if he wasn't there he would drive
into Gordon and check out the bars. It shouldn't be
hard to find him in Gordon, for he had been told
there were only two bars in the town and one of
them didn't much like having Indians in the place.
The name of that place was the Stockman Bar. The
Indian bar was the Silver Spur.

He had no difficulty finding the Desmet place.
It was on the northwest side of Gordon about ten

miles out of town. He got to the ranch about one
P.M. and it was then hotter than the devil, he
thought. Much hotter than when he had started out
from Rosebud Reservation. It had to be nearly 100°
and the strong wind was, if anything, now blowing
harder.

As he drove up the long drive he saw a man
come out of the ranch house on top of the hill. The
man was very tall and he carried a rifle. It must be
Desmet. There weren't very many men around any
taller than Roger.

He introduced himself, reminding Roger they
had met briefly at Rosebud months before.

"I was with Elijah Black Horse," he began a
bit hesitantly, not saying what he had planned to
say and that was, I am a friend of Elijah Black
Horse. He didn't know how upset this man was.
He had heard from Doris Mae, but he knew
how truthful she could be when the mood suited
her.

"Sure I remember," Desmet said, smiling. It
wasn't a smile that came easy. He put the rifle to
his side and behind him as if he was embarrassed
that he had carried the weapon with him at all.

"You know, I reckon he ain't here anymore,
and I don't want him back. Matter of fact, I will run
him off if he comes back."

Bennion said nothing, thinking only that the

trouble must have been big to have the usual calm Desmet this upset.

"Things that bad, are they?" Bennion said, wishing he hadn't said such a silly thing as soon as the words were out of his mouth.

"That bad and worse. Very bad. As bad as they can get. Really used me, that Indian did. Put me half-way through summer with no good chance of getting another man. I don't need to tell you how bad that is."

Bennion nodded his head that he understood. But the man wasn't through yet.

"And that wife of his, she's no better. Worse maybe. Sometimes I think she was the real cause of the trouble over here."

"I saw her yesterday," Bennion said. "That's how come I'm here. 'Course I didn't know what to believe, she said so many crazy things."

"Black Horse beat her up," Bennion went on. "What a mess! I never saw anybody worse beat up than that woman."

"Nobody deserves that kind of beating," Desmet said. "But if I had to pick out somebody who had to be beat up bad like that I swear I would pick that woman. I suppose that's terrible for me to say, but she sure can try a man. More than any Indian woman, or man, I ever did know."

He smiled and Bennion began to feel better

about being around the man—more at ease, anyway.

"No sense standing out here in the hot sun. Come on in and sit for a while and I will give you the whole story."

Bennion wasn't sure he wanted to hear the whole story. He had heard enough already but he didn't want to leave right away. He had just arrived. And besides, it was awfully hot where they were. The house looked invitingly cool with all those shade trees around it, and, once inside, there was a tall glass of lemonade waiting. Desmet went on to tell the story in all its ugly details. He didn't leave out anything and Bennion didn't interrupt him. The man clearly needed to talk and tell somebody what had happened. He finished by saying how he was sure going to miss that Indian in spite of all that had gone on, and how impossible it would be to replace him and how Black Horse had been doing so well for so long and he still didn't quite understand what went wrong. It all happened so fast, he said, that he wasn't even aware there was trouble building.

On the ride into Gordon Bennion thought sadly how this kind of experience for the Desmet family did nothing to improve already bad Indian-white relations. Heaven knew those relations sorely needed mending, too. Never more than recently.

He wasn't so sure anymore, though, that much of anything could be done to improve the way the two people got along. But then he felt that way only at his darkest moments and now wasn't exactly a high point. Maybe it was the heat and all the unpleasant news that affected him this way. Land was the center of the controversy, he knew. It had always been the land, even if it was like this dust bowl of a ranch. The Indian had recently become much more conscious and protective of his land base and the outside threats to it and that, in turn, angered many whites who leased Indian lands and ran cattle on the leased sections. These Indian lands, reservation lands, came at an ever-increasing price to whites, which only made matters worse. But not only were the Indians protecting what they already owned, or was held in trust for them, they were now clamoring for more land. Trying to expand their holdings through court actions and treaty rights. Whites, on the other hand, had lived for years with the hope that if not they, then at least their children would live to see the day the reservation system was dismantled and the land sold for what it would bring and to the highest bidder. And they were confident it would go to enterprising hard-working local whites who were about the only ones who put the land to good use anyway. Now, however, the reverse was a possibility, if something less than a certainty. And with the land, or the claim of the land, came power and influence, and as a consequence of this growing power there was a backlash from the whites in the region. In fact, not just in the region but in the West itself. At least that was how Bennion saw it all unfolding, and it promised to be an ugly business.

19

HE FOUND THE Silver Spur with no problem. It struck him peculiar that it was called the Silver Spur, for there was no sign anywhere to suggest or even hint that the place had a name, much less a colorful one like the Silver Spur. In his mind the Silver Spur evoked a picture of a gambling casino like one he might see in Reno, with beautiful women and bright lights.

Gordon in many ways reminded him of Valentine, Nebraska, although smaller. Its main street ran north and south. As did most towns in that area of Nebraska, Gordon existed almost entirely as a shopping place for the families who farmed and ranched and the Indians who came to shop from Pine Ridge Reservation.

He was somewhat nervous about going into the bar. He had been in bars before, but not very many, a few here and there, although he would not have cared to admit this to the Mormons he worked with. They would be shocked beyond words if they knew or even suspected he enjoyed a cold beer on a hot dry day.

Nobody paid any special attention to him as he entered. The barkeep looked up but then returned to whatever he was doing. He must have looked like any young rancher who came in out of the sun for a cold beer. There was no way anyone could pick him out as a Mormon. He didn't look the part. He was hot and he knew his face and neck had burned on the drive over from the reservation. His face often burned in the summer because of his light skin. No pigment in your skin, Pappy told him. His hair was blond but was turning brown as he got older, and worse than that, it was quickly getting thinner, falling out. He hated to admit it, but it was. He wore a gray Stetson hat that he didn't take off when he entered. His face was moon-shaped, but it was the smile that practically snuck across his face that people remembered about him. It was sometimes described as a cunning smile that turned into a grin as he stood watching something or someone and thinking, while chewing on a toothpick.

There were both Indians and whites in the place, but not very many in the front section by the door. He couldn't see who was beyond the lattice-work partition in the back but he could hear voices and music from the music box. The light wasn't good and it took him a while to adjust to the darkness.

He walked to the bar on the left and took off his hat and put it on the bar and said hello to a cowboy standing a few feet away and nodded at the barkeep. The barkeep was a thin man with thin red hair who was wearing a candy-striped vest that made Bennion think of a circus barker he had seen once when his pappy took him to a circus in Salt Lake one Saturday. "Step right up, folks," the man had said.

The barkeep came over immediately. "What can I get for you, young fellow?" he asked in a friendly voice.

Bennion ordered a Grain Belt beer. In a minute a cold bottle of beer stood before him on the counter. He looked at it for a long time, trying to remember when last he had had a bottle of beer. Two years before, he decided, as he picked up the bottle and took a long swallow. There was nothing in his opinion that curbed a strong thirst on a warm day like a cold bottle of beer.

Something in the back behind the partition was occupying the attention of the barman. He kept trying to see above or around the latticework where the voices of several persons and loud laughter could be heard. He was talking about the people behind the wall to the cowboy, but Bennion couldn't hear the words. The way both kept turning and twisting to see what was going on told him they were interested, even worried, about what was happening.

Must be Indians, Bennion thought, and they are nervous about what is going on back there where they can't be watched. He finished his beer and started for the back section where he guessed the men's room would be.

Beyond the latticework wall the room was much darker, but his eyes quickly adjusted to the dim light and he could see fairly well. There was a table of Indians in back, all quite drunk. Two women and three men, with one man so drunk his head was hanging in a way that made it appear he might fall off the chair at any moment. Bennion stood there a moment studying the group, waiting for the man to lift his head. When he did, Bennion recognized Black Horse. He had never seen his friend so drunk and he was undecided what to do.

Go out the door and go home, something told him, but he didn't. He stood there watching the Indians. As he watched, Black Horse recovered somewhat and was suddenly alert and waving his hands and talking all at the same time. It was peculiar. One minute he looked like he was about to fall off his chair and the next he was so alert he was almost jumping around.

One of the women at the table was young and pretty. Eighteen, maybe younger, he thought, while the other woman looked like a slightly older Doris Mae. She had no teeth and was very worn in appearance. There were also a young man who was quite drunk, his head nodding as though he, too, was about to pass out, and a much older man with a large red nose. He might have been the young man's father.

No point getting involved in this scene, Bennion thought, and he turned to walk back to the bar when Black Horse saw him and stood up as if to get a better view and be sure who it was he was seeing. He hadn't expected to see Bennion, no more than Bennion had expected to be there.

"Is that you, Jim Bennion?" Black Horse hollered so loud that the barkeep and the cowboy at the bar stopped talking and began gawking, again trying to see around the latticework.

He laughed when he was sure it was Bennion.

150

"Come over here, you son of a gun. Come over and meet my good friends. Have a drink with us. I know you don't drink, Jim, but one little beer won't hurt you none."

Another of those peculiar laughs punctuated his conversation. Bennion had a feeling that the laugh had nothing to do with how Black Horse was feeling. It didn't mean he was happy.

Bennion walked over to the table and pulled up a chair and sat down.

"What are you doing over here, Jim?" Black Horse asked. "I know, don't tell me." And then there was a laugh again. "Doris Mae sent you over to get me. Right? How is good ol' Doris Mae anyway?" He laughed again.

"Nobody sent me," Bennion said, a bit annoyed. And in a way, what he said was correct. He hadn't been sent. He had come of his own accord. Nobody sent him anyplace. Certainly not Doris Mae.

"I thought I would run over here and see how you're doing. Yes, I met Doris Mae in Corn Creek. She's staying at your mother's place."

"And the kids, they okay?" Black Horse asked.

"Yeah, they're okay."

Then there was another of those laughs that Bennion could only describe as inappropriate because nothing even remotely funny had been said.

Sometimes nothing at all was said, but the laugh came out anyway.

Nothing I can do here, Bennion decided, and he was about to get up and leave when Black Horse leaped to his feet and said in a loud voice: "I want you to meet my good friend, Jim Bennion. Jim is a real good friend to the Indian people."

He patted Bennion on the shoulder and looked at him long enough for Bennion to see his eyes, which were red and swollen. And he looked as if he had been in a fight, too. His face was bruised and lumpy. He wondered how long it had been since Black Horse had slept.

Bennion was embarrassed with the attention he was getting. He wanted to leave quickly.

"Jim Bennion came to Corn Creek last summer." Then Black Horse stopped as if he had forgotten to explain something.

"Why, I plumb forgot to tell you good folks that my friend here is a Mormon elder all the way from Utah. That right, Jim?"

There was that laugh again.

"Elder Bennion it is. Sometimes I forget myself because he is the damndest most un-Mormon-like fella you ever met. Not like the others. Does he look like a Mormon to you?"

Nobody was listening to Black Horse. The two women were chatting away about something important to them. The young Indian boy was weaving in his chair, about to fall on the floor unconscious, and the old man was kind of staring off into space, not looking at anything or anyone.

But that didn't stop Black Horse. He kept talking.

"Elder Bennion here is so good to me that he lets me paint pictures in his room over on the reservation. I even have my own key." And as if to prove he did, he stood up and began fumbling in his pockets for the key to show everyone.

The drunk idiot, Bennion thought. I had better get the hell out of here quick.

Black Horse had been almost screaming as he told this story about his friend Elder Bennion, and the commotion brought the barman around in a fast trot, as if he might be arriving just in time to head off trouble. It was difficult to see, however, how such a scrawny man might stop four or five determined Indians from doing anything they cared to do.

When Black Horse saw the barman, he hollered at him. "Hey, mister, come here! Bring my friend Elder Bennion a drink. Bring us all drinks." He waved a ten-dollar bill in front of the barman as if to say, see, I have the money to pay. The barkeep was satisfied and left to get another round for the table. Then he put in a call to the sheriff's office, explaining that there wasn't yet any emergency, but he had an Indian here who was pretty drunk and looked like he might become trouble fairly soon, and would they please send somebody around to quiet the man down and get him out without a big fuss if that became necessary.

Sheriff Abe Pates arrived alone about fifteen minutes later. Bennion was about to leave the table, not having touched the second bottle of Grain Belt, when he heard the angry voice of the sheriff behind him. He turned to see a man with gray pants and a nightstick in his hand and a revolver on his belt standing there glaring at Black Horse.

"I warned you, mister, to stay out of this place. You mustn't understand English good." He ignored everybody else and looked straight at Black Horse, who acted as if the sheriff hadn't come in, but he saw the sheriff, all right.

Black Horse called out for the barman to bring another round with one for the sheriff.

"I ain't drinking your liquor, Indian," the sheriff said, not softening a bit in his approach or taking his eyes from Black Horse.

"I am not fooling with you, mister. I don't want you in this place or for that matter in this town. Now, you come along with me quiet-like and the rest of you get the hell out of here."

154

He motioned with his nightstick, and the Indians at the table fled in all directions except for Black Horse. Bennion began to move away too, but as he got up he thought he might convince the sheriff to allow him to take Black Horse on back to the reservation with him. He was going home right away anyway.

He thought later it was a foolish idea, for the sheriff, being alone and remembering how tough the Indian Black Horse had been the last time they arrested him, was quite nervous, and so when Bennion moved toward him to try to explain his idea, the sheriff misunderstood the move and came around with his club hard aside Bennion's neck, knocking him to the floor. The sheriff then turned, for not much more than a few seconds, to see where Bennion had landed and to determine, presumably, that he was indeed out of the way and no threat. In that second, Black Horse came across the table at him, wrestled the nightstick from him, and got him on the floor and underneath him. From somewhere he produced a pocketknife that he opened and plunged into the chest of the struggling Abe Pates. The blade pierced the tip of the man's heart. In a few minutes he was dead. It had all happened so fast and the knife was so small nobody thought the sheriff was hurt seriously. Then the cowboy who had pulled Black Horse away, the one standing at the bar, looked down at the sheriff and saw the knife still in the man's chest.

"The son of a bitch knifed the sheriff," he hollered, and suddenly there were cries from whites to kill the Indian. But the barkeep, Ramon, quick-thinking and cool, prevented more violence by immediately calling in for more help and, as they all waited for help to arrive, talking quietly to the white men there, saying how he thought the sheriff might still be alive and that if the Indian was killed, all hell would break loose in the town.

This was a real consideration for Ramon. He was half owner in the place and he didn't fancy the idea of running a bar that did business mostly with Indian clientele that had allowed white men to murder an Indian in his bar. The Indians would get revenge for that. He had seen it before.

Finally help did arrive, the two large deputies who were off doing something else when the call first came in. In the confusion that followed as they tried to determine if Abe Pates was dead or alive, Black Horse pulled away from the cowboy who held him and ran out the door into the alley and disappeared. A couple of men went after him but the others stayed behind, confident he would not get very far. Besides, they had Abe Pates to worry about now. One man said, "The hell with the Indian." Another said, "We will get him later."

Black Horse, they thought, would head north for the reservation, and he did. So they knew where to look for him when the time was right. But a man could cut across the countryside, and under the cover of darkness pursuers would have one hell of a time finding him. When it got light, though, he should be easy to see from the air. There wasn't much cover between Gordon and Rosebud, and what cover there might be in a wet year was gone now with three years of drought.

Jim Bennion knew none of this. He lay unconscious. In a few minutes he was carried off to the Gordon jail and kept there that night and most of the next day until Roger Desmet heard of the death of Abe Pates and came into the office to inquire about the Mormon Bennion. He had a strong feeling Bennion had become involved in the trouble.

Roger spoke with a confused and somewhat nervous deputy, a man he didn't know very well. The man was kind of in charge now and apparently was catching hell from all directions. The white ranchers wanted revenge for the killing of Abe Pates. Blood for blood, they said. And yet the deputy didn't want something to happen to the one prisoner he did have. The young man back there might not have done the actual killing, but he was involved, maybe even caused the entire affair by his hanging around with the Indians, he told Roger

Desmet. That alone was enough to keep him in jail for a while. Still, he was awfully nervous that a gang might come for the young man and that he then would be forced to deal with something extra legal, like a hanging. He wanted no part of that business. But people were plenty stirred up about Indians.

Roger said to him, "You know this guy you have in there is a Mormon elder?"

The deputy looked up at him, puzzled as to what that meant. "So?" he said.

"So it might be very unwise to keep him very long since he had nothing to do with the killin'. They will get the Indian. Probably the highway patrol has him already. Why do you want to keep the Mormon? It don't make good sense to me, 'specially since you have to worry something might happen to him all the time he's in here."

"I am keepin' him 'cause he might be part of this murder. I don't know that he ain't. I've had no chance to talk to him or anybody else. Damn phone rings all the time, or people keep comin' in to hear what's goin' on."

"If something happens to that boy you will have the Mormon Church down your back as well as who knows who else. Those Mormons are mighty powerful people," Desmet said.

Al Tumble—that was the man's name—didn't

know much about the Mormon Church, but he had heard the usual stories. Stories about their money and influence and stories about how clannish they were. He supposed he didn't want trouble with the likes of them. The Indians were enough trouble all at one time.

"Why, those Mormons can't be as bad as the militants we get in from Rapid City—they're plain loco. They don't use an ounce of common sense, I tell you. The Mormons can't be that bad, are they?"

"That's the point, Al, you don't want a bunch of militant Indians in from Rapid City and at the same time answering all the questions of officials from the Mormon Church. You will be a hell of a lot busier then than now, that's for sure. It don't make good sense to me to keep the Mormon. We know where he is. I mean, he is just over the line in South Dakota. He won't be going far."

"Just over the line, you kidding? He might as well be in another country once he gets back to that reservation. We don't have any say over there. I don't know what to do. I will have to make some calls, and then we will see."

Roger knew who would be making the decision. The mayor.

He left, but when he called back that same afternoon, as he said he would, to see what they were going to do, he was told by Tumble that the decision had been made to release the Mormon, provided the young man would get the hell out of Gordon—indeed, out of Nebraska—and back across the line to South Dakota and the reservation. That hardly sounded like a condition to Roger. He guessed Bennion would be more than happy to get back home to the reservation once he was out of jail.

About an hour before the scheduled release, Desmet went to the jail again. He was supposed to be the only person told that the Mormon was to be let go, but he wasn't sure he was. He wanted to be there, he said, to explain to Bennion, although he hoped it wasn't necessary, that he best not waste any time in getting back onto the reservation. He would stress the dangers that awaited him should he linger. Bennion didn't need to be told this, however. He understood quite well what was happening and what might happen if he were not very, very careful.

Along about ten P.M. Bennion was released, let out the back way. Roger drove Bennion's station wagon around back for him. There was to be a police car following him at a respectable distance until he reached the South Dakota line and then he would be on his own. "You go like hell from then on," Roger said. "Don't look back." It wasn't until Bennion was released and had talked with Roger that he understood Black Horse had escaped. He had thought Black Horse was in another cell, or perhaps in another jail.

The police car stayed with him at the same distance until he reached the state line and crossed into South Dakota and then the patrol car stopped. The headlights grew small as Bennion sped up on the open and deserted highway headed north toward Rosebud Reservation.

The road ahead was darker than he remembered it on other nights and oncoming traffic made him nervous, but not nearly so nervous as the ones that came up behind him and passed him by. He had convinced himself there was a gang of shotgun-carrying cowboys somewhere near Gordon waiting to follow him out of town and do their worst, whatever that might be. He didn't want to think what they might do to a fellow who was friendly with an Indian who had just killed a white sheriff. Suddenly a large car came up behind him and passed him as if he was not moving. But that vehicle, what he saw of it, looked to him to be a Cadillac. It was white and big, he saw that much, and had orange or yellow plates. California, he guessed. There was only one person in the vehicle. Probably somebody barreling across the country from one coast to the other. The rest of the way back he saw only one other vehicle and it was no threat. He was close to the reservation line now and figured if anyone planned to come after him they would have done so before he got so close to home. There was no sign on this end of the reservation, but he knew when he was on the reserve, even if nobody else would.

He looked out on the darkened prairie and wondered about his friend Black Horse. Where was he now? Indeed, where would he have gone had he been in his place? Home to the reservation was a sure bet, and the police would know that too. And Black Horse would know they knew, but that wouldn't keep him away. There was no place else for an Indian on the run to go, no place where there would be familiar land and people he knew and could trust. In time they would get him and have to send him back. There would be a federal warrant for his arrest. Interstate flight, it would be called, or something like that.

Was the news yet in Corn Creek? he wondered. News like this traveled fast. He supposed all bad news everywhere moved like hell. Now he could see the lights of Corn Creek ahead. They stood out like a beacon on the seashore, only this was no seashore. Far from it.

If anything, he drove faster toward those lights, the lights that made him feel warm and as if he belonged someplace, and he supposed he did, however brief his stay might be now. He thought some more about what he would say to Doris Mae and the others who would want to know everything about what had happened in Gordon and why. He didn't think much about what he would tell the other Mormons. That seemed almost unimportant, although he knew he would have to have an explanation, for they would be asking, and asking soon. What mattered to him was what he would say to Elijah's mother, Helen, and Doris Mae and Lester Leader Charge, the community chairman, and so many others who would want to know the ugly details. How this awful thing came to happen. What was the reason for the violence? they would ask. And what would he say? Only the truth. There was nothing else that could be said. But what was the truth and who was to blame? That was harder for him to decide.

He drove into town, not knowing what to expect in the way of a reception. But as usual, the place was quiet and sleepy, as it almost always was after eleven, especially on a week night. Now it was after midnight and he supposed it would have been quite an extraordinary sight to see lots of people milling around waiting for the Mormon Jim Bennion to return and to hear his weak explanation for the trouble he had caused over in Nebraska. That was how he had pictured the scene as he drove home. It wasn't that way, however. There were no angry crowds. There were no crowds at all.

The road into Corn Creek from the state highway is gravel and rocky in places and washed out in other places. A driver must be careful at night. He picked his way along slowly. It was still hot, above 80°, he was certain.

On his door was a letter pinned to the wood and he swallowed hard when he saw the return address: Rosebud, South Dakota, Church of the Latter Day Saints. They've heard already, he thought. And they've been out to see me, too. How did the news spread this fast? he wondered. He pulled off the letter angrily and let himself into his room. The note wasn't what he expected at all. They didn't know after all. He felt like laughing. Elder Stimpson had written the letter. He was angry about having had to drive all the way out to Corn Creek and then not finding Elder Bennion at home. He went on to say that a replacement, a partner, another Mormon, had arrived on the reservation and was to be sent out to Corn Creek to join Bennion that very week, or as soon as possible. He was also told to call Rosebud as soon as he came in. The new elder's name was Fielding.

Bennion threw the letter in the wastebasket. Served Stimpson right to come out here without calling. But he knew why Stimpson and others did this. They wanted to find him doing something he shouldn't, or else not doing anything at all, which was even more likely.

How unimportant it all seemed to him now. It was almost funny that after all that had happened in the past twelve hours he should come home to find a letter giving him hell for not being home when one of the other elders came calling. How he wished he had been home now. All the usual nonsense Elder Stimpson would have had to say would have been much better than what had actually happened in Gordon.

He made himself a cup of tea. He knew he wouldn't be able to sleep right off, and then he shut off the lights so somebody wandering around the village, some drunk probably, wouldn't see his light and decide to pay a late-night call. Only the drunks did things like that. He needed time to think. And he needed time to decide what he would tell the people of Corn Creek about Gordon and what had happened over there. He stared for a long time at the blue flame under the teakettle, wide awake as he tried for the hundredth time to determine how things went so wrong so fast.

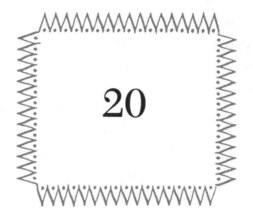

20

BLACK HORSE HID. Then he traveled some. The whole state and federal police forces were mobilizing to hunt him down, he imagined. In fact, not that many police were out after him but more all the time were being called up to help in the search. But now he was free and he was walking and he was not afraid, or not as afraid as he had been when he scrambled out of that bar hours earlier. Then it was sheer terror that carried him out of Gordon. And as on other occasions, like the previous winter, there was tranquillity in being alone in the night, only this time there was no snow and it wasn't cold.

Traveling over the land, it was surprisingly cool for such hot weather. The land was not familiar, but in another sense he felt as if he knew it, and he felt strong and sober. He headed north in the direction the reservation lay. He was sure the law officers would expect him to go this way, but that didn't dissuade him. He would go there just the same. The only haven he could imagine was on the reservation. The night was clear and the stars overhead made the light almost too bright for someone not wishing to be seen. But he saw no signs of a search for him, although he was certain they were out there or would be when the light was better. The search would begin in earnest in the morning with the first light. Then he would have plenty to fear and no time to enjoy the land.

It had all happened so fast, it was as if it hadn't happened at all. He couldn't quite believe he had killed a man, not even that cruel sheriff, but he knew he had. He had heard the white men shout that the sheriff was dead. It frightened him more than anything in his life. Had he meant to actually kill the man? He did it, so he guessed he had, but it was more an uncontrolled drunken rage that made him do it, than anything else. And Jim Bennion. What of that poor fellow? They couldn't be keeping him long, he thought, but was he seriously injured by the clubbing Abe Pates gave him? As he thought of that beating his anger returned, but less strong now. And what might the white ranchers do to him? Not a person like Desmet, of course—he wouldn't harm anybody, but there were plenty of others around Gordon who would. Desmet was a fair man and he felt regret about the way he had treated him. It had been a rotten payment for kindness. He considered Desmet's offer of a job and a place to live that summer the act of a friend, and he hadn't repaid the help with appropriate behavior. It had all turned out so bad, and so different from what he had expected or wanted, but now it was much too late to do anything except run and escape, if he could. He knew what he would face should they catch up to him. A lifetime in a Nebraska jail if they didn't decide to go ahead and kill him and say he was trying to run away. That sort of thing wasn't unheard of. No, jail in Nebraska was more than he could deal with now or any time. He would keep running as long as he could.

Why hadn't that fool sheriff used better sense and stayed away from him? He was only trying to prove something and what did it get him, get either of them? Chief Acorn in Mission would never have done such a foolish thing. He knew better. He knew how to handle liquored-up Indians and with much less force, too. But this fellow Pates was downright brutal. Still, that didn't justify what he did. Nothing could. That was the horror of it for him.

My God, he thought again. Now it is murder. It has gone that far. Before, he was a drunk, sometimes a disagreeable drunk. But he was a drunk who didn't or hadn't gone around killing people. Now he had. He was little better than Little Bald Eagle and others like him who he had told Doris Mae were evil and to be avoided. And to think he had bragged to Bennion how all the whiskey and wine in his life had not brought him so low that he had never needed to beg. And now he had gone so much lower and killed a man.

And Doris Mae. Where was she? he wondered. Back on the reservation, he hoped. She too wouldn't be very safe in and around Gordon, and yet she might not have the good sense to run away. She would not use common sense if she thought he was still in jail there. But somebody would have to have told her by now that he wasn't. There was no place else for Doris Mae except the reservation. He had been foolish and mistaken to think there was, and he wished he hadn't taken her away from there. And he wished even more he himself hadn't left and had to be making his way back home in this fashion, in the still of the night and as a fugitive.

The reservation police, he knew, would concentrate their search in and around Corn Creek, for they would expect that in time he would go home. But the only safe place for him was the reservation. They knew the Indian had to go home to the reservation. It was simply a matter of time and waiting. But there were lots of places he could hide on the reservation and the police knew this too and would want to keep him from making the reservation line. And state police in Nebraska would be especially interested in finding him before he reached the reservation boundary, for they had no jurisdiction on an Indian reservation, a federal reserve. But that wouldn't keep the tribal and federal police from hunting him down like a dog, but it wouldn't be as hard for him on the reserve. He had friends there, and even those people who were not friends might not turn him away, for they knew what he was feeling. They might pretend not to see him as he passed by. He couldn't count on this, for there were also persons who would turn on him immediately if he gave them a chance or there was the promise of a reward. He had to avoid those persons.

Now he was just thinking and walking and trying to follow the contours of a dried-out creek bed that appeared to be meandering its way north across open, treeless land that would have been dangerous for him to travel by day. He listened and he smelled the night air and he stopped to try to hear motors overhead, like from a helicopter, but there was only silence. Yet in all of this there was peacefulness. It was as if things now were as they should be, even though he realized they wouldn't remain that way for very long. It was only a matter of a few hours before it would be dawn and the activity picked up. There would be Nebraska police and probably the FBI and who knew what other police out there, all after him.

He stopped and listened again. He thought he heard something, but there was no sound. Then he heard it again and smiled. It was the bark of a coyote, and then a second coyote, maybe answering the first. Then a third. They were fairly close, he guessed. It was comforting to know the coyotes were out there.

"So you're out there again, Mr. Coyote," he muttered. He thought of what his father had told him: the coyote teaches the Indian how not to be captured. He felt like lying down and going to sleep, although he couldn't risk that. He had much too far to go before the light came up.

Morning came and he was hungry and very tired and miles from nowhere. He rested some, hiding among the scrub trees along a creek bed that no longer had water rushing through it. He hoped he couldn't be seen, but he knew that whoever was out there looking for him would be following the creek bed with aircraft, for it presented about the only cover for miles. He could feel the hot sun and it was severe even under the low bush, but he didn't move very much and pretty soon he was asleep. Once he heard the motor of a small airplane flying low and he was sure it was searching for him, but he didn't stir and soon the motor was hard to hear. He felt thankful and would have prayed, but he couldn't. He didn't know what to pray for, save his own survival. Still, he felt the need to pray. He was very frightened.

On the radio and television in the area the news was out. The broadcaster said a dangerous, cold-blooded killer was on the loose and he was an Indian. An Indian murderer on the loose. Photographs of Black Horse's face were on TV for citizens to memorize. People locked doors where they hadn't before. Men checked their rifles and shotguns. There was considerable fear.

"Cooperate with your local police," the TV advised. "If you see this face, contact the nearest law enforcement agency."

Now it was night and Black Horse was walking again. The night was black and he was thankful

172

that it was. It must have been what he was praying for, he thought. He had no good idea of where he was, but he knew he had to be nearer the reservation. He felt like some of the countryside was less strange, although he couldn't quite call it familiar either. It was not land he had recently walked across, but then, it had been years since he had ventured very far from the highways on the reservation the way he used to. Yet there had been a time he remembered when, as a young man, he and his first wife had hiked across the prairie far from roads and settlements and people, hunting for old burial grounds his father had told him about as a boy. He didn't remember ever finding those burial sites, but then, they wouldn't have known if they had, he thought much later, for the grass would have grown over the area. But at the time they never thought about those things. They just kept hunting as if they would actually find the sacred grounds on the next rise. Along the way they would often lie in the tall grass and watch the deer that were plentiful then and they would creep up on them to see how close they might get before their scent was caught and the deer bolted and ran. They saw possums, too, and prairie dogs by the hundreds. Sometimes they would come upon prairie-dog towns that stretched about as far as he could see. That seldom happened now, however, with the land fenced. Anyway, cattle land, grazing land, was much too valuable to allow prairie dogs to dig up the countryside like a bunch of gophers. And aside from ruining good grazing land, it was dangerous for the stock to pick their way across the land with all those holes. So those days county agents, men like Roger Desmet, were sent out to poison prairie dogs.

And the birds they saw in those times he just didn't see anymore. He guessed they were still around, but he couldn't remember seeing any recently, at least not anywhere near the highways. But in those days there were grouse and pheasant aplenty. Now the pheasant population around the reservation had to be protected and the hunting season limited for fear the hunters would wipe out the bird population. Poachers, too, were a constant problem on the reservation the year round.

But that was all so long ago. He was so young, not even eighteen, and she a year younger than he. Ah, but so wise for her years, he remembered. He had barely known her when they got married, but he loved her like nobody since. And the way they came to marry seemed funny now, although he hadn't thought it so funny then. Her father married them off, insisted with gun in hand that they get married before Black Horse went off to the service. And so they got married before he left for the army.

The funny part for him was that she wasn't even pregnant. But it had been a good thing the old man had insisted with the gun, for he might not have done it if the decision were left up to him. Matter of fact, he knew he wouldn't. He needed some direction in those days and the gun was about all it took. He never regretted marrying that girl. She was gentle and she didn't drink, either, but he did his share even back then. He drank her share, he supposed. He never was told what she died from. All he knew was that she died while he was away from the reservation with the army. He never saw her again after he left for the service. Later he heard she was killed in a car wreck.

It was a year or two after he got back that he met up with Laurene and they got married. She was a good woman also and gave him two children before she died, and they did many good things together. Traveled a lot and saw so many things, but before he knew her very well she was gone. Died of some sickness that winter, one of many who were to die that year.

And now there was Doris Mae. Perhaps the last. How different were his years with her, not that he could blame her for what happened. She was okay in her own way. She did the best she could. She wasn't the one who did anything to him. But how things had changed. How different he was from the boy who enjoyed lying in the tall grass observing the wildlife of the land. Now there was no more time for that. The gentle things that were part of his life weren't there anymore. They had been replaced with moving around back and forth to the reservation, too much drinking, and too much time spent in off-reservation border towns like Gordon and a string of others like them in South Dakota and Nebraska and North Dakota and Wyoming. Wherever there were Indians. And Doris Mae his companion some of the time, matching him drink for drink. He didn't even understand why she stayed, nor did he understand why he kept going around with her. It hadn't been good for either of them. And now this awful trouble.

Black Horse walked on. He was thinking and walking all the night through. This was the second night in a row. He listened and he smelled, as if trying to be sure that every moment was full and experienced. Even though his hunger was considerable, he was moving fast. He must have covered thirty miles, he figured, and so long as he was headed north he should be getting close to the reservation boundary. It was a good night to travel and he hoped a good night to make his escape. He was surprised that he had not seen more activity in the air above or behind him, but so far all was quiet. Still, he knew the police, be they reservation or state officials in Nebraska, would surely kill him this time if they had the chance. He intended to see that they didn't. He knew they were tired of arresting him for drunkenness and assault and then seeing him out within a few days. Now they had something big on him and they had an excuse to kill him. They wouldn't want to have him live and risk having him go free again. That's what they would think might happen if they didn't see him dead this time.

He was trotting now. Sometime toward morning he began to itch, and there were little bumps on his arms and he wondered if he had lain in poison ivy or poison oak. There were loads of that poison stuff along the creek bottom.

He stopped and looked around. The morning wasn't far away. He took in deep breaths, trying to relax and keep his head. He took stock of his physical condition. He felt pretty good, if not exactly strong, and the hunger was less on his mind. Yet he knew he must eat soon in order to continue to keep going at this pace. How long would he need to continue traveling? Another night, perhaps two?

He had come upon some trees along the border of a farm. Then he crossed a road into open farmland. He was taking risks because the sun was coming up and he could be spotted out in the open. But there was a farmhouse not far away and he hoped there might be something he could eat near the house, maybe a little something, even if it was garbage, to keep him going. He crept up to the back fence on his belly. There was no sound, nor did the house appear inhabited. He looked at his hands and arms as he crept closer. They were cut and bruised and there were more of those lumps from the poison ivy, or whatever it was that he had been in. He could see some rubbish and a garbage pail or trash can and he was moving toward it. When he saw the rubbish he decided the house must be lived in. He was almost to the back door of the house when he heard a shot. He turned around on his stomach, afraid to move and afraid the next shot would hit him. In the distance he saw the figure of a farmer in overalls coming toward him and hollering and waving the rifle.

Black Horse got to his feet and ran and saw the man lift the rifle and take aim. He wasn't a good shot, but then too, Black Horse was moving fast. The explosion of the gun told him it wasn't a big rifle. Probably a squirrel gun, but he had respect for any gun. A small caliber could kill mighty well. He went down a slope and behind the trees that were on the edge of the man's property. He was surprised to see he was on the outskirts of St. Francis community, which was on the reservation. He had come far. He was out of Nebraska, across the state line and on the reservation, for whatever good that would do him.

The next hours were quite unforgettable, for within a half hour there was a sky full of aircraft, and if he hadn't been so near to St. Francis he would surely have been captured in that time. But the half hour he had before the aircraft were zooming overhead every which way was enough to make it to the old water tower that served St. Francis Mission. There were two water towers in the town. One new, a golf-ball type, high and modern and close to town. It served the needs of the St. Francis community. The other was older, it belonged to St. Francis Mission. It was perhaps fifty feet high and looked to have no way to climb onto except for some steel webbing under the tower. But a man climbing up through that maze could easily be seen and the tower had no outside ladders on the structure itself, so obviously a man could not climb the outside of the tower. That part was true, but Black Horse knew something he hoped the police didn't, and that was that the tower was under repair, at least it had been weeks before while he was in jail at Rosebud, when he had been sent as part of a jail work crew to clean out the inside of the tower. Then prisoners had to climb the rigging to a door and into the tank itself, and once inside, scrub the tank floor and walls. Only three men went up that time. The others were too afraid of the heights. But he had been one of the three and he knew the way into the bottom of the tower, a tower that no longer held any water. He hoped that those walking underneath didn't know this. He climbed the rigging faster than he would have thought possible and quickly was at the small door that he hoped like hell wouldn't be locked. There was no point in locking it, he figured, for even the most daring of kids wouldn't climb onto this tower. He saw right away that work was still going on inside. Some kind of patching job. It was very dark inside and he couldn't hear any noises from outside, not even the aircraft overhead. He felt safe in his hiding place, if only the police didn't arrive with dogs. Dogs would lead the police right to the base of the tower. But they didn't arrive with dogs. The search teams moved into St. Francis community itself, going from house to house. But now it was only federal officers, for Nebraska authorities had no jurisdiction here. That night, near to eleven o'clock, he climbed from the tower and walked into St. Francis community well-satisfied with himself but also about falling down from exhaustion and hunger. When a man passed him in the street he staggered like he was drunk and turned away so he wouldn't be recognized. But the man who passed didn't act as if he was on the lookout for anyone. He just glanced at Black Horse as if he were another drunk, and there were plenty of these in St. Francis all the time. He found an abandoned house where there had been a fire. He slept for a few hours on the floor of that house. It felt good to be able to stretch out. But he didn't dare remain there long, for he needed what darkness there was to get out of St. Francis and close to the Little White River, where there was good cover and land he knew well. The nearest spot to intersect the Little White River was outside Spring Creek, and that was a good eight or nine miles more of walking. The eight miles to the Little White River wouldn't be so much to do, he decided, provided he could find something to eat, and he was sure he could do that in St. Francis. But he had to be very careful. Finally he took a chance and went into the all-night service station to see if he might buy a few bars of candy out of the vending machines. He had money he kept in his shoe. No change, however. So that meant asking the attendant for change and risking being identified. But the attendant was asleep. Not just asleep, but passed-out drunk at the cash register. Black Horse picked out a couple of quarters from the cash box and bought his candy and walked off into the darkness behind the garage, headed west toward the Little White. The man in the garage had not stirred or made a sound. Black

Horse munched on the candy bars, thankful to have them. A cup of coffee would have been even more welcome, but there was no way he could have that, not this night.

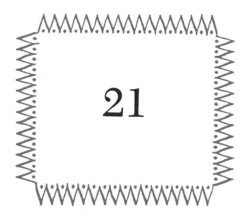

21

FOR A FEW DAYS visitors coming around to see Bennion had a lot of questions about what had happened in Gordon. Then the visits stopped
altogether. It was a clear message, or ought to have
been, anyway, that he wasn't welcome in Corn
Creek anymore, although nobody came out and
said this to his face, not right then. But he knew he
was being frozen out, ignored, not spoken to on the
street, and in this way being told he was no longer
considered a friend to the Indian people and that
maybe he ought to go home, or if not home, at least
someplace away from Corn Creek.

183

No tribal official came to see him to say any of this. He was kind of expecting a visit any day. Tribal officials were less subtle than the people about what they wanted, especially the tribal president, Featherman. He would say outright that he didn't want somebody on his reservation and expected that that somebody would get off the reservation about as quick as he could. Finally, one morning, the community chairman for Corn Creek, Lester Leader Charge, did come around and, over a cup of coffee Bennion provided, he advised ever so politely that Bennion ought to be making his plans for leaving before something bad happened. He didn't say what that something bad would be, but he didn't have to. Bennion had a rich imagination. Leader Charge told how he had received a call from the tribal president, Amos Featherman, and that while he had not given the direct order for Bennion to leave, he was a bit concerned for the Mormon's safety in Corn Creek. Leader Charge then explained how the next message from the people of Corn Creek might take an uglier form and not be merely the silent treatment he was now getting. It might be some kind of direct threat, he said, and if he didn't pay attention to a threat, then about anything might happen. He could make no guarantees, he said, if Bennion stayed on too long. He was truly sorry, he told him, and that this was nothing

184

personal. Bennion believed the man meant every word he said. Clearly he was not comfortable saying the things he felt he had to say. He liked Leader Charge. That was the problem about leaving. He liked almost everybody he had dealt with out there in Corn Creek, even, in a way, Doris Mae. He was coming to understand her better now, for whatever good that would do, he thought. None that he could see.

"In a couple of days," Bennion said to the community chairman. "I will leave Corn Creek in a few days." The chairman nodded his head that he understood, but he said nothing. As he prepared to leave, Leader Charge again apologized for having to come and tell Bennion this news. Bennion waved off the apology. "I understand, Lester," he said. "I really do. And I appreciate your warning me, and I will be leaving soon. That's a promise."

That night the warning Leader Charge and others had talked about came. It came as a gunshot in the night. Somebody shot a small-caliber rifle, he guessed a .22 rifle, through his window. The shot was high, very high on purpose, he liked to believe, and that made him feel a bit easier, for he figured whoever it was didn't aim to hit him, not this time anyway. Of course he had to recognize that the gunman could have been just a lousy shot or was drunk and not seeing all that well. But such

185

thoughts didn't comfort him much. He was fairly sure he knew who had shot out his window. His name was Tuffy Bordeaux, a seventeen-year-old boy in the community whom he knew quite well. Only that very day Tuffy had come to his door, the first visit in days, to warn him that the people of Corn Creek were fed up with the Mormons and him especially, and they wanted him to get out of town pronto. Tuffy liked the chance to play this kind of role, Bennion knew, but he doubted that Tuffy actually spoke for the community in any meaningful way or that he had any information that suggested the people in the town were demanding he leave, even though he knew plenty wanted him out and out as soon as possible. But Tuffy was known to have done things like this before, and Tuffy had been drinking and Bennion was sure he owned a .22 rifle used to hunt squirrel and prairie dogs. But if he was wrong about Tuffy, or the shot had been made by somebody else, he was risking a lot. Or maybe Tuffy or somebody else would try again, and if the shot hit him the next time, he knew a .22 slug could kill mighty well. So he might be in real danger after all, but still he stayed on or thought he would anyway, for he had no place else to go unless he left the reservation or moved in with the other elders at Rosebud and he wouldn't do that. He felt he couldn't stand that.

He didn't report the incident of the gunshot to the tribal police, for he knew what they would say —get out of town for his own safety. Besides, they would surely relate the incident to the tribal president and he might become much more direct about Bennion getting off the reservation for his own safety. For now, however, he would stay, he told himself, feeling brave.

But the gunshot incident wasn't nearly as upsetting to Bennion as what took place when he met Doris Mae in front of the post office in Corn Creek.

He had considered the possibility of meeting up with her, but he told himself he wouldn't be a prisoner in his own room. He would have to see her sometime. Still, he wasn't prepared for her rage.

He passed by her and went into the post office and she said something uncomplimentary, although he didn't know what, because she spoke in Indian. But he knew she was speaking to him and the laughter from the Indians standing nearby convinced him that whatever was said was not very friendly. A crowd had gathered. And when he came out with his mail she spat at him. The spit ran off the toe of his boot. He looked at it, then at her, and walked away, but she wasn't letting him go that easy.

"You're no damn good, Jim Bennion!" she

screamed after him, in English now. He walked toward the grocery store.

"A no-good fucker." She spat again.

Then she said something in Indian and everybody laughed again. She was a little drunk, he thought.

"Preacher man who is supposed to come to help us poor Indians and all you do is buy drinks for Indians and try to go to bed with their women."

A damn lie, he thought, but he could see she had heard the latest rumors too. She would add to the stories, give them a new dimension, but what she was saying now was very, very damaging. People who might not otherwise believe the rumors would believe Doris Mae. She, after all, should know, shouldn't she? Black Horse painted at Bennion's place. They were good friends, and so whatever Doris Mae knew or said she knew had to be the truth. Her informal street testimony meant the end for him in Corn Creek.

She kept on talking, adding more to the stories as she went along.

"I know you real good, Jim Bennion. All the time buying whiskey for Elijah so he can't come home to me. So he would stay and paint his pictures at your house for you to sell and give the money to your church. You made Elijah get drunk and kill the white man 'cause you were mad that he wouldn't paint no more pictures for you to sell for your church. You done this, Jim Bennion. Elder Bennion," she spat out the word Elder with hatred.

"You Mormons are no good...." Her voice trailed off as he entered Dillon's Market. Al Dillon, the son of the owner of the store, was behind the counter. He was about thirty, dark and overweight and balding, and to Bennion he looked older than he was.

"Turn on you every time," he said. He had watched the scene as it had unfolded in front of the post office. He felt genuinely sad for Elder Bennion, although he had seen similar things before and had warned people, including Elder Bennion, but they didn't often believe him.

"You can't trust them. I try to tell people when they first come here, but usually they don't listen. The Indians are like children. They're okay until something goes wrong and they can't have their own way. Then watch out.

"I deal with them in here all the time. I've worked with them, lived next door to them, grew up with them, gone to school with a few of them, and I've never seen anything change much. Oh, every few years the government comes in with a crash program to make things better—like building new houses or spruce up the reservation—but in a short while everything is like this again." He spread his arms out to take in Corn Creek. "A slum."

Bennion watched him but didn't say anything. It had been a while since anybody had been in to do any sprucing, as Dillon liked to call it.

"You missionaries come here to try to change them but it can't be done. They won't let it. Nothing is ever going to be any different for them until the reservation is broken up and they are made to go out and earn like the rest of us and pay taxes and accept the responsibilities that come with living in this country. Nobody gets a free ride."

That was it with these white people who lectured him about Indians. A free ride. They were afraid the Indian was having a free ride and they were jealous and pissed-off and who knew what more.

Bennion made his purchases but Dillon didn't keep quiet.

"You wait. I bet when they get your friend Black Horse, he gets off easy. The whites in Nebraska will want to handle him with kid gloves— you can put your money on that. They won't want crazy Indians invading their towns like we have over here in South Dakota."

Bennion left. He thought about what Dillon had to say and went home. Doris Mae was nowhere in sight.

22

IT WAS WELL AFTER midnight when the two white
men reached the edge of Corn Creek, the north
side. They parked the dark-colored sedan and got
out.

One of the two men was tall and lean and
boyish-looking in his horn-rimmed glasses and
short blond hair. He was about twenty-five. The
other man was shorter and older and a good deal
heavier. He was forty-five. The way the taller man
followed the older, it was clear who was in charge.
Neither man wore a uniform, although both were
Nebraska Highway Patrol officers.

"My God, isn't it dark," the younger man said.

The other man didn't answer. Dark it was, though. Away from the main streets in these reservation towns there were no street lights, and since most homes had no electricity there was not much light at all. But the man knew where he was going. He had scouted the locale earlier, when it was still light.

"From here on you say nothing, Frank. I will do whatever talking there is to do. Understand?" This from the older man.

"Sure, Ed. It is your deal. I am just along to help however I can."

Ed Carter carried a flashlight, but he didn't wish to use it unless necessary. When he reached the Black Horse cabin it was so dark and there were so many dark forms in the fenced-in yard that he had to shine the light around the yard. All that he saw was clutter, including a car seat near the cabin door.

Once he had his direction, the rest happened fast the way he had planned for it to happen. He pushed open the cabin door, which wasn't locked —there were no locks on most doors in Corn Creek—and barged in, gun drawn while the younger officer stayed in the yard to cover him from behind and see that nobody escaped through a window or rear exit. But in fact the one window in the cabin was boarded up and there was no rear door.

"All right, get up. This is the police," Carter ordered, his voice high-pitched and excited. "We're looking for Elijah Black Horse." He shone the light around the cabin, which was small, only a room and a half.

"He ain't here," came a frightened reply from Helen Black Horse. She was telling the truth too. Thank God, she thought. Her voice was amazingly calm.

The cabin was full of people, nine in all. Doris Mae and her two children were there, although it is doubtful that Carter knew who she was. He hadn't bothered to learn much about Black Horse's family. He didn't care anything about them. Also there were Victoria and her two children and Helen Black Horse, of course, and several relatives from another community.

Carter saw mostly women and children as he scanned the cabin with his flashlight. There was one old man, but he certainly wasn't Elijah Black Horse.

Then came the excited voice of the other officer from outside.

"Ed, I got one out here. Don't you move, mister, or I will shoot you. Don't try anything. Now, get out of that car!"

He had found Two Teeth asleep in his car. Two Teeth climbed out of the back seat, confused and frightened. He thought they were being robbed, but he couldn't imagine why, for they had nothing. Less than most people in the village. When he was away from the car where Frank could see him well, and see that he had no weapon, Frank quickly put the man's arms behind him and handcuffed him and pushed him through the cabin door in with the others. Carter was waiting at the cabin door and he tripped Two Teeth so that he fell face first with a thud. Fortunately his face hit the mattress on the floor and he wasn't injured. Carter next put a gun to the head of Two Teeth, cocked it, and asked. "This man's name Black Horse? Somebody tell me quick before I shoot him. Is this Elijah Black Horse?"

Victoria Two Teeth screamed and moved toward her husband, whom she thought was injured, but the other officer was now in the cabin too and he stepped in front of her and pushed her away. When she came back a second time he clipped her with the handle of his revolver. This sent her scurrying into a corner, crying and holding her right eye. Doris Mae made no moves. She sat quietly and watched.

"Now, I ask you again, is this man Elijah Black Horse?" Carter was quite sure it wasn't, even in the darkness, but he was going to get someone there to tell him this or he might shoot the bastard.

"He is my son-in-law," Helen Black Horse said in that same calm voice. She was anything but calm inside, however.

"His name is Lyle Two Teeth," she said. "He don't do anything to anyone," she said. "Don't hurt him, please. He don't understand good." What she was saying was he was mildly retarded.

"You think I ought to kill this bird?" Carter said to the younger officer, who was a bit surprised with the question. He didn't know what to say. He didn't understand that they would kill anyone unless they got lucky and found Black Horse and he tried to escape, which was unlikely. They were here, he thought, to shake down the people for information. Nothing more.

He didn't answer and apparently Carter wasn't looking for a reply, for he seemed to forget Two Teeth for a moment and told his assistant to get him one of the kids.

He shone the light on Denise, Black Horse's little girl, although Carter probably didn't know who she was. Terror was in the child's eyes and she clung to her mother, but the young man pulled her away and over to where Carter stood. He took her arm and held it hard.

"You want to see this child grow up, do you?"

He cocked his police revolver again and held it to the head of the child who, while frightened, didn't quite understand what was happening.

"Who are these people?" Helen Black Horse said in Indian to Doris Mae.

"Police from Nebraska," she said.

"What are you two jabbering about?" Carter demanded to know. "If you care anything about this child you will tell us where that murderer is. If I find him I am going to kill him just like he killed my friend Abe Pates."

Actually, Carter barely knew Abe Pates and didn't especially like the man the few times he had had to deal with him. But Pates was a police officer and that was what was important now.

"I suggest you get wise before somebody gets hurt."

The calm was gone from Helen Black Horse now. She pleaded. "Please don't hurt that child. Hurt me, but not the child. She's done nothing."

She tried to get up off the mattress but she couldn't. At night in the damp cabin she could barely move, her arthritis was so bad.

The younger police officer was beginning to be concerned about this assignment. He was about to say to his superior, "Enough, Ed. Let's get out of here. They know nothing," but he didn't have to say this, for car lights filled the cabin. It was merely a car passing by on the way to another cabin, but it was enough to spook the already agitated Carter and so he released the child and told the other officer to take off the handcuffs from Two Teeth.

"You better not hide your son, old woman, for we will come back if we hear he's hereabouts. Next time somebody could get seriously hurt.

He kicked Two Teeth in the side and told him to get up, which he did slowly, half expecting to be pushed down again, but this didn't happen.

Then they left, leaving a thoroughly terrorized and confused Black Horse family. Helen Black Horse didn't know what to do. She knew these men couldn't be connected with the tribal police. She had never seen tribal police, even the worst of them, act like this and for no good reason. She feared for her son's life now more than ever before. She knew men like these wouldn't easily give up and she knew as well that the tribal officials would be almost powerless to stop this kind of thing from happening again.

23

ONCE BLACK HORSE got to the banks of the Little White River it was easy to travel. He made his way along the river bank past Grass Mountain and on past what was known as Crow Eagle's Paradise. At Crow Eagle's he figured there would be persons sympathetic to his troubles, but at the same time he knew that would be one of the first places the police would look for him. Federal authorities were sure to be watching Crow Eagle's camp, no doubt expecting Black Horse to appear there if he were to go anywhere on the reservation other than Corn Creek. The truth was that he hardly knew any of the political people who hung about that pretty set-tlement along the Little White. He knew only what everybody else on the reservation said, and that was that Crow Eagle's camp was the center of the activities of the militants and the activist types on the reservation, and that didn't describe him in spite of all that had happened. He didn't know those kinds of people. So when he got near the camp he carefully circled wide in case there were police posted near the river bank. He knew how jumpy a police officer might be, having been dropped anywhere near Crow Eagle's camp and told to wait there. The police were plenty afraid of Crow Eagle and the people who hung around the camp.

What Black Horse didn't know and had no way of knowing was that when his arrest and escape be-came known around the reservation the word went out that an Indian was being hunted by the federal authorities and Nebraska police, who had no busi-ness on the reservation. And that he would need help. And the best thing anybody could do was to become highly visible by hiking out onto the prairie away from the settlements or to drive their cars to remote areas of the reservation so the au-thorities might be kept busy chasing after the wrong Indians. Indians in considerable numbers were out of their homes, wandering around in unusual places, more visible, although apparently not many considered the hazards in doing this. No one thought he might be shot by mistake. The police stopped any number of persons they thought was the Indian Black Horse, miles and miles from settlements, but in each case that person proved to be somebody else.

Black Horse in the meantime stayed close to the Little White River, moving north toward White River community. The cover was good along the Little White. One night he spent among campers in Ghost Hawk Park, a favorite campsite for white tourists. He came up from the river bank after dark and told the white people he was a fisherman, but wanted to sit among them a while and talk if they wished to have his company. Of course, they were delighted to have a real live Indian at their campfire and food was offered and, at last, hot coffee. While among the whites at Ghost Hawk Park he considered and rejected a way to escape from the reservation. He could catch a ride in one of the recreation vehicles the white people drove, and once away from the reservation travel would be relatively easy. But where in the world would he go? He didn't have any idea whatsoever, so gave up the plan, deciding instead to stay along the Little White.

He had a vague notion he might stay with an

uncle in the Indian section of Mission, a place called Antelope community. Antelope was a growing subdivision of Mission Town. It was at times a rowdy, noisy place, full of fighting drunks. The police were always out there, but Black Horse figured he might go undetected there amid the usual din. He wouldn't be looked for in Antelope, no more than any other place.

His uncle, a man by the name of Tiny Roubideaux, was a well-known character around Mission. A well-known drunk, that is to say. He had a big mouth and was prone to be violent when he was drunk, which was often, but he was also a generous sort and to be trusted.

Anyway, this was about the only thing he could think to do as he made his way along the river south toward Mission Town. He would have liked to go home to Corn Creek but he knew that was plain crazy. He would be watched for there, and who knew what kind of trouble his appearance would bring for his mother and Doris Mae and the others? Maybe if he got his bearing at Mission Town and some cash, he could somehow get a message to Doris Mae and the others. Doris Mae could meet him in Denver or Casper, Wyoming, or someplace like that, far from the reservation. She would be afraid to go so far alone, but he figured she would do it if he told her how.

He followed the river north about as far as he could before it swung away from Mission Town, Then, walking as fast as he could and staying low, he cut across the open land heading directly for Mission Town, then went round the center and east toward Antelope, about two miles on the edge of Mission.

Antelope is built on tribal land, while much of Mission Town isn't. So Antelope came under the tribal law enforcement and not the police from Mission. It meant that town police were supposed to have no authority there, but they were out there plenty because the trouble was more than the tribal police could handle on busy weekends. It got so bad sometimes that the trouble spilled into Mission Town itself, and when it appeared that was about to happen, the Mission Town police helped all they could.

Tiny lived in one of the new houses the federal government had built in Antelope. Actually, before all the federal building, Antelope was much smaller and quieter. It was a shantytown then. Now there were lots of new houses. Some well kept, a lot more showing early wear and decay. Somehow Tiny had qualified for one of the new houses. It wasn't all that much of a mystery that he had got one, but to hear some people talk you would think it was. When Tiny had got his big house, he had a wife and five or six kids living with him and no-body needed a house more than he did. Now he had nobody living there with him, having long since kicked out his wife and kids when he caught her with another man. And as if that wasn't waste enough with so many needing ade-quate housing, he hadn't paid any rent on the place for months, but still he stayed on. Some said it was because he was so ornery and the offi-cials in the housing office were afraid of him, which might have been true.

It was late when Black Horse got to the house he thought belonged to Tiny. The place was dark and, not surprising, the door was un-locked, so he let himself in and went to a back bedroom where he found a mattress on the floor. That was all the furniture in the room. In fact, there wasn't much furniture in the whole house that he could see, but then, he couldn't see very well, for there was no electricity in the place. There were lights and wires to the house, but Tiny had stopped paying the Cherry Creek Elec-tric Company light bill and they weren't nearly so charitable about carrying him as was the housing authority. The room he picked for himself wasn't the one Tiny was using. He made damn sure of that. He wouldn't want to be asleep and have the man stagger into the room and find him there. He might do about anything then. He smiled when he thought that a person could easily live in this big house for a week without Tiny even knowing he was there. It was clear Tiny wasn't around very much, and when he did come home it was to sleep off a drunk. There wasn't much food in the house and so Black Horse ate what little he had carried with him when he left the white people at Ghost Hawk Park. It wasn't much, and he was hungry as he lay on the whiskey-reeking mattress. The mattress smelled like somebody had thrown up on it at one time, which he knew was entirely possible.

He didn't sleep well. Every sound—and there were many in Antelope—had him up on his feet peering out the window. He was beginning to believe coming to Antelope might have been a mistake. Yet he wanted to be in touch with Doris Mae and his mother to let them know he was alive, if nothing else, and he thought doing this from Antelope was about the best chance he had.

A rattling at the door had him on his feet and then crouching low to see into the other room. Somebody had come in but he couldn't see who. But whoever it was was alone and acted like he knew where he was going and had done this kind of thing before. He moved around the house quietly as if he knew where everything was. Then

Black Horse heard cursing and talking like there was someone else out there, but he was fairly sure there wasn't. He knew it was his uncle Tiny. He was very drunk. In a few minutes the moving around stopped and there was silence. He figured the man had gone to bed. He was probably near passed-out drunk anyway and was alseep about the time he hit the mattress. He heard nothing more until morning, and when he got up he found that his uncle was still asleep, but he must have been a fairly light sleeper, for when Black Horse began moving around the kitchen trying, unsuccessfully, to find something to eat he heard Tiny call out in a loud voice.

"Who's there?" he said with no worry in his voice, like having someone poking around his kitchen in the morning wasn't all that strange. When Black Horse didn't answer right away, Tiny was on his feet and into the kitchen rubbing his eyes and then the back of his head.

"Well, what have we got here?" he said. "Where in hell you come from? I don't remember you here last night. Then, I can't say I remember last night all that good." He smiled. He and Black Horse generally got on well. Others in the family didn't, however.

"You come in this morning or last night?"

"Last night. I was here when you come in. I

didn't want to worry you none by comin' out of the room back there, so I went back to sleep."

They spoke in English. He wasn't sure Tiny even knew any Indian. Maybe a few words, but not much more. He hadn't grown up with the Indian language the way Black Horse had, even though they grew up a couple of miles from each other and there wasn't much difference in age. Tiny was five or six years older, he guessed.

The name Tiny hardly fitted the man, for he was anything but. He was, in fact, quite the opposite—big, gigantic really. He was a good six foot four and weighed in at about 250 pounds. He had large coarse features and a heavy beard that was almost black. It wasn't that he didn't shave; he did. Still, his beard was black an hour after he shaved. Among Sioux Indians, who usually had little or no body hair, a heavy beard was unusual. But then, Tiny was only about half Indian, maybe less.

The rest was French blood, his grandfather on his mother's side having come down from Canada and marrying a Sioux girl who was probably not a full-blood either.

"So what is this we been hearin' about you, Elijah?" He liked to call him Elijah. Others called him Eli or Black Horse, but not Tiny.

"It's real bad, Tiny. Police everywhere lookin' for me and I am plumb wore out. I been living along the Little White River where the cover is good."

"And so you thought of your ol' uncle, did you? I don't know if I should be proud or mad with ya. Police finds ya here and they gonna arrest me for helping ya. Some of them police fellas would like nuthin' better'n get reason to arrest me, aside from being drunk. Anybody see ya come here?"

"I don't think so. It was dark and there was lots of people runnin' around here. This place is sure busy late at night."

"This place is crazy all the time, Elijah. Nuthin' like it was before the new houses got built. Then it was mostly quiet, not like now with the fightin' and killin' and the police out here more than anyplace on the reservation.

"You hear about the LaFollette boy?" He didn't wait for a reply from Black Horse.

"The kid went and hung hisself yesterday. He was in the Mission Town jail. I don't think he was more'n eighteen. Just went and hung hisself with shoelaces. How do you figure somethin' like that, Elijah? You tell me. I mean why? It weren't like the police done anything much to him. Sure he was in the lockup, but that was nuthin', 'cause he only got caught breakin' into somebody's house with another kid. For that he wouldn't face no time. Shit, he would have been out in a day or two. Still, he up and hangs hisself, and with shoelaces, no less. Ya wouldn't think somebody could hang hisself that way, would ya?"

The suicide clearly had Tiny befuddled and about as upset about anything as this unusually calm man got.

"But ya don't wanna hear about this town, Elijah. I could talk about it all night, the things that go on around here. Ya got trouble enough without hearin' about other people's woes. We got to figure out what to do with ya. Ya can stay here for a couple of days, and probably nobody goin' to know any better, but folks around here poke in other people's business pretty regular, more'n you'd think, and someone sure as hell would find ya out, and with the turncoats we got around here, it wouldn't be no time 'fore the police would be down on ya, and me too, I guess." He laughed when he said that.

"Let's make somethin' to eat and think on what we can do with ya. There ought'a be a safe place for you on this big reservation. Until things quiet down, I mean, and they will quiet down, ya know. People forget and get busy doin' other things."

And so they ate. Black Horse prepared the cold meal from some cans Tiny got from his room. They talked about what might be a safe escape route. Finally Tiny said, "I know. Milk's Camp. We will hide ya out at Milk's Camp."

Black Horse knew of Milk's Camp. Knew where it was, but that was about all. He hadn't ever been there, for it was over a hundred miles from Mission Town, and while it was part of the reservation, there being reserve land there, it was outside present-day reservation boundaries by many miles.

Then Tiny explained. He had a friend by the name of Bad Whipple who lived out at Milk's Camp and operated a motel called the Deer Crossing. It was a combination of a café and motel, and from what Tiny said about Whipple, this half-breed Indian did quite well with his business enterprises. He had several others on and off the reservation, including a ranch near Mission someplace, which somebody else operated for him, and part ownership in a café near Winner, South Dakota, off the reservation.

Black Horse never quite understood how it was that Tiny and Bad Whipple were such good friends, for he was quick to see that two more different men couldn't be found. Where Whipple was quiet and very industrious and a nondrinker, Tiny was the opposite. A heavy drinker and loud and known to be violent when drinking. But they were friends, there was no mistaking that fact. Perhaps it had something to do with time they had spent together in Vietnam. Maybe something happened there, but Black Horse didn't ask.

Tiny called Whipple and said he had a nephew who needed a place to stay in a bad way and how he would be no trouble and he ought to put him in a room where there wasn't a lot of traffic so he wouldn't be seen much, and that he wouldn't be going out while there. Now, any fool would know something was wrong in such a situation, but Bad Whipple said bring him round when you're ready, and so Tiny did. The next afternoon they drove out to Milk's Camp and Black Horse wondered if the beat-up pickup truck with practically no muffler would get them there safely. And he worried about the breakneck speed that Tiny drove that wreck, but above all else he worried about being stopped by a South Dakota Highway Patrol officer, for off-reservation police were constantly on the lookout for reservation vehicles. It was common knowledge that reservation Indians ran around without license plates or insurance. Tiny was no different. He would not have had the money to insure his truck even if an insurer could be found. They didn't get stopped, however, and they got to Milk's Camp without incident.

The post office for Milk's Camp is a place called St. Charles, South Dakota, a white community. Milk's Camp itself is spread out, with no real center except for a picnic park near the Catholic church located almost on the banks of the Niobrara River.

Milk's Camp is quite hilly and is surrounded by much rich wheatland. Officially, it is part of the Rosebud Sioux Tribal Reservation and there are about thirty-five to forty families living there.

Milk's Camp got its name because Chief Milk had used the spot as a camp many years before as the Sioux band moved from the Missouri River site on their way inward to a spot at Rosebud, the new reservation.

Tiny's friend Bad met them at the door of the office to the motel. He saw them drive up. The Deer Crossing Motel was near the river but not very near any of the houses in Milk's Camp. It was a run-down-looking establishment, badly in need of repairs, but there were shade trees aplenty and the spot looked cool to Black Horse on this hot day. A neon sign that read Deer Crossing had several letters punched out. It looked like someone had shot out the sign with a rifle.

Bad Whipple was also a big man, but not nearly as large as Tiny and he weighed much less. Still, he was big and he had dark hair cut short in a military-style clip and his face was burned brown from the sun. He looked like he worked outside a lot. He was in his early forties and could have passed for much younger if he were somewhat lighter.

If Bad Whipple recognized Black Horse, he didn't indicate that he had. There was a very brief

211

introduction, with Tiny saying only that this was his nephew, and with Black Horse putting his name down as Reggie Sharp Fish. Bad said nothing. He asked no questions.

He had to have put it all together by now, Black Horse thought, hoping like hell the man could be trusted as much as Tiny said he could. But he had no choice, he decided—he had to trust the man, for he simply had to stay someplace for a while and this place was a considerable improvement on the Little White River.

Tiny came up with about twenty bucks, which was half a week's rent at the Deer Crossing, and he promised Bad the rest as soon as he got back to the reservation. With this done, Black Horse was installed in a small but very adequate room in the back, away from what little traffic there was this time of year in the motel. It was understood that Black Horse would take care of his own linens—they would be left outside his door. This wasn't such an unusual arrangement, for many construction people stayed at this motel, and to save money they took care of their own linens and in this way got a cheaper rate.

"I'm gonna go see your mother when I get back," Tiny told Black Horse as he got ready to leave. "Ya got anything ya want me to tell her? I will tell her ya okay and out here. Is that all right?"

Black Horse shook his head. It was okay.

"You tell her I am good and tell Doris Mae too. Maybe Doris Mae she can come stay here a while."

Tiny frowned but Black Horse didn't notice.

He didn't think he would tell Doris Mae anything. He wasn't sure she could keep her mouth shut.

"We gotta be very careful, Elijah," Tiny said, thinking how if Doris Mae got drunk she might say too much and by accident might reveal where it was Black Horse was hiding. But he didn't say any of this to Black Horse.

"Your mama got any money she's holding for you, Elijah? Bad will keep ya here long as I say so, maybe he will even wait for his money, but it ain't fair to ask the man to keep ya for nuthin'. He's not goin' to buy food for ya, I'm sure."

"I don't know what she's got. She ain't keepin' money for me, I know that. But she might have some of her own. Some saved up. I'm pretty sure she would give you that."

Before Tiny drove back to the reservation he cut Black Horse's hair, which was now quite long. He cut it very short, almost as short as an army haircut grown in a little. It looked kind of funny but it changed the way Black Horse looked a great deal, and that was good, Tiny figured. They joked about changing the color of his hair, maybe to

213

bright red, but both knew that would be plain insane.

"Now, ya can trust Bad. Remember that, Elijah. No matter what happens, trust him. He won't do nuthin' to get ya in trouble, but he can't do much to help either. I mean ya gotta keep him out of any trouble if it comes out here. Understand?"

Black Horse did. He felt better to hear Tiny say again that Bad Whipple was dependable. He sure wondered what it was between them that made Tiny so sure of this half-breed Indian Whipple.

"And you'll have to stay inside all the time, and I reckon that won't be so easy after a while. Be by yourself most of the time. Go out to buy food or have Bad buy it, but bring it back here to eat. Don't stay out where ya be seen. Ya got some money left for some food? I don't have any left."

He did. He had about twelve bucks left from what he had carried away from Desmet's place in Gordon. Tiny promised to be back in a few days with more money and some food if he could manage it.

Tiny left, reminding Black Horse again that from what he had heard on the TV the police from Nebraska were still hunting him hard.

Except for going out for some food shopping, and then not for long, Black Horse stayed in the room and nobody came around, and this went on for nearly a month, with Tiny visiting about every week. The first week he had money for him. Said he got it from Black Horse's mother and that she was so very happy he was okay. When Black Horse asked about Doris Mae and the kids, Tiny told him they were okay and were asking for him, but in fact he didn't know this. He had spoken only to Helen Black Horse and made sure she was alone and told her he thought it best not to tell others, even Doris Mae.

"So when is Doris Mae comin' to visit me?" Black Horse asked. "When she gets here I figure we will make plans to leave. Maybe go on up around Wyoming someplace. Away from here."

"I think things is quiet'n down some," Tiny said. "There ain't much huntin' for ya goin' on around the reservation, best I can tell."

That was true, although Tiny failed to say the Nebraska police were still hunting Black Horse, nor did he tell Black Horse about the men who went to see his mother and had terrorized the family. And those two men, he had heard, had visited other relatives of Black Horse on the reservation and he wouldn't have been very surprised if they came looking for him, except he was ready for them if they did. His shotgun was loaded and near his bed so that if they came through his door unin-

215

vited, like they did with the others, they would get one hell of a surprise and that would be both barrels right in the face. But they didn't come around, perhaps having been warned that Tiny Roubideaux was big and mean and no man to trifle with. It made him angry when he thought of two white police from off the reservation working their will the way they did. Oh sure, he understood they came in the night, under the cover of darkness, but that didn't excuse the tribal police and the federal police from stopping this kind of activity. He guessed the tribal police didn't care, or didn't care enough to do anything much about it.

Sometimes Tiny got drunk and didn't get to Milk's Camp with the food and money he was supposed to bring. One week he spent the money Helen Black Horse gave him and got himself crazy drunk. That week, Black Horse, out of desperation, had to go to Bad Whipple for money for food. He gave him the money. He didn't seem to like the idea, but he gave him the cash just the same. Bad was a funny guy, Black Horse decided. Most of the time, though, Tiny was fairly reliable about getting to Milk's Camp to see Black Horse and to carry with him what he needed in food or money.

Things went along in this way through the fall and into December, until one day Black Horse felt he just had to get out of the room that had become a prison as bad as any he had imagined awaited him in Nebraska. Even with the TV and comforts he was sure weren't in prisons, he felt trapped and very very alone. So it was while feeling this way that he slipped out the rear of the motel and walked along the bank of the Niobrara River. He walked until he saw a shack about a quarter of a mile up the river. At that point he would turn around and go back rather than risk being seen. Nobody saw him, he was certain, and so he began to make this same trip each afternoon, sometimes taking a pencil and paper and sketching things that interested him. The cover was good and he didn't fear being detected. Besides, he decided, nobody was looking for him to be in Milk's Camp.

It was on about the second or third of these short walks that he was noticed by a woman by the name of Ellen No Moccasin. She lived in the shack by the river that he saw but never approached. She watched him sit on the shore and draw his pictures. Her interest at first was mere curiosity, but when he reappeared day after day her interest grew. One day she got a good look at him through field glasses she had borrowed from a neighbor. For several days she watched Black Horse through these glasses, not recognizing him and deciding he wasn't anybody she knew from Milk's Camp.

One night while watching TV and a news wrap-up she saw a picture of Black Horse flashed on the screen and realized immediately that the man on the river was the Indian fugitive Black Horse. The man's hair was shorter and he was lighter, she could see that, but she was sure it was the same person.

There was no mention of a reward on the TV but she remembered reading of a reward when first he was sought by the Nebraska police. She grew excited thinking of the things the money might buy, like a refrigerator she desperately needed, the old one having stopped running the month before. There was no money to buy another.

The next day she had one of her sons follow Black Horse at a safe distance to see where he was staying. She had already guessed he was at the Deer Crossing but she wanted to be certain so there would be no hitch to her receiving any reward offered. Then she made her call to Gordon, Nebraska, not revealing anything until she was assured the $1500 reward was still being offered and that she would get every penny if her information led to the capture of Black Horse. And she was further promised that her part in the capture would not be made public. She could collect her reward, the man said, and nobody need know anything of her role. It was made very simple for her and so she told what she knew and the voice on the other end of the line got very excited with the news. She could tell this by the way the man thanked her and thanked her, again and again.

24

IT HAD BEEN a quiet evening and Bad Whipple decided to close early and go to bed. The café had already closed for lack of business. Now he was about to shut off the outside motel sign. The place wasn't half full and he knew it wasn't about to get busy. This wasn't the time of the year for much traffic for the motel. He was alone in the small motel office, his wife away for the evening. Just as he was about to lock the office door two white men approached, ordinary-enough-looking fellows, and strangers. On closer examination, however, and in better light he knew they were police officers and he guessed why they had come. He said nothing, however. The older officer was a man about his own age, while the younger fellow looked like a kid. The young guy was quite agitated about something; the older man cool and in control, like he was a person who knew what he wanted to do.

The older man spoke, identifying himself as a Nebraska police officer and showing a badge and giving his name as Ed Carter. He didn't give a name for his partner.

"We're looking for an Indian, mister, and we hear he is here. You know anything about that, do you? I expect you don't have very many of them in here."

"Exactly two," Bad said. He didn't like the man. "Unless, of course, you count myself, and then you got three."

The white man ignored the comment but Bad knew the man looked at him again. He had, no doubt, known few Indians who ran businesses.

The officer produced a picture of Black Horse.

"Which room?" the man demanded. He was very sure of himself and very sure Black Horse was here. He didn't even ask how Black Horse was registered. He seemed not to care at all whether Bad knew this man or he didn't. All he wanted to know was which room held Black Horse.

"He's in seventeen," Bad said. "In the back."

"Give me the key."

"Look, I don't know what this fella suppose to have done, but why don't you let me call him up here and you can take him. Arrest him, I mean. He don't seem like a violent man to me. He would go quiet, I am certain."

The officer smiled a nervous smile. Now he was getting excited. Apparently his mind was racing ahead to what he had to do and he wasn't hearing what Bad suggested.

"Just the key, mister." He pulled out his gun, not to threaten Bad but to examine it as if to see that it was right, but Bad knew why the gun was shown. It was to remind him he had better give over that key if he didn't want trouble of his own. He handed the man the key.

The man moved quickly down the hall toward the back and to room 17.

The other man started to follow him but Carter said, "No, I will handle this myself. You stay with the Indian." He meant Bad. "See that there ain't any warning phone calls. We don't want that son of a bitch knowing I'm coming."

The hand in which he held the gun now shook and the young man noticed this and grew more nervous himself. Again he wished he wasn't a part of this investigation, but knew it was much too late to get out of what was to follow. He would be involved, very involved. It was clear to him now that

Carter had been working himself up to this moment for a long time. All those visits to the family of Black Horse had served as a stimulus for what he would do now.

What came next didn't take very long. In a matter of moments there were two shots fired and the Nebraska officer was back even more shaken up than before.

"He threw something in my face. A soft drink, I think it was. I had to shoot him. You better call an ambulance."

An ambulance came in about ten minutes and during that time Carter would not allow Bad to go back to see how the injured man was. When Bad insisted, Carter pointed the gun at him and said, "No. You stay here with us." He did.

Black Horse was shot twice in the chest. He lay alone in a pool of blood, moaning and groaning. The TV was on and a late movie playing. He died a few minutes before the ambulance arrived.

Bad Whipple knew what this was all about even before he discovered there was no soft drink or anything else on the floor and Black Horse had no weapon in his back pocket, as was later claimed by Officer Carter. He regarded the shooting simply an eye for an eye and a tooth for a tooth situation. Nothing more. The Nebraska police had their revenge.

25

THERE WERE MANY questions following Black Horse's death. What, for example, was the Nebraska Highway Patrol doing in South Dakota and why weren't the South Dakota officials advised of the pending arrest, and did this action take place on tribal land where the police had no jurisdiction? There were few clear answers to any of the questions except for the jurisdiction issue. The Deer Crossing Motel was near tribal land but not on it, and so jurisdiction proved not an issue at all.

Bennion read of Black Horse's death in the *Rapid City Journal*. He was by this time spending most of his time in Mission Town, although the leadership of the Mormon Church wanted him away from the reservation. But he wouldn't go. He wasn't doing anything now, but he wouldn't leave until something was settled, as he knew it would be sometime soon. He kept his room out at Corn Creek but was seldom there since the gunshot in the night, the gunshot he was sure came from Tuffy Bordeaux. Now he lived with another elder at Mission.

The charges of foul play were very real, Bennion suspected, and so did everybody else on the reservation, and the attorneys general of both states were calling for an investigation of the incident, with the Nebraska Highway Patrol claiming at a press conference that "We wanted to put him on trial. We wanted more than anything to take him alive." But nobody really believed these statements. They didn't want that at all and nobody was more vocal about this than Tiny Roubideaux. He said, "I feel they wanted him kilt and done it their way."

All very true, Bennion thought. But nothing much will come of any of this. He had come to accept, more than he liked to admit, the injustice that was part of the life on the reservation in South Dakota. A year before he would have been jumping up and down demanding an investigation. That something be done. Now he was quiet. He said nothing. He prepared to leave the reservation, the something he was waiting for now having arrived. He couldn't quite bring himself to feel sad. He felt bad, but not sad. He would have felt much much worse had Black Horse been captured and given a lifetime of jail in Nebraska. That would have made him feel immeasurably worse, but there was no way to explain his feelings to anyone around him now. He kept his thoughts to himself.

He could have another mission, he was promised by Church officials. The offer wasn't made, he knew, because he was such a good missionary. Anything but. The truth was that the Church was having increasing difficulties getting young men to take the missionary experience seriously and so there were openings galore everywhere in the West.

He went to the traditional wake at the Legion Hall at Corn Creek. He went with apprehension, fearing an encounter with Doris Mae, but there was none. He considered going over to say a few words to Helen Black Horse, but he didn't. He didn't know what he would say, so he sat there alone having good thoughts about Black Horse. He tried to remember the happy times. That, after all, was why they had all gathered there in the hall. To remember the good things. For some reason,

though, he kept remembering something that had
happened when he first got to know Black Horse.
Word had been given to Black Horse that an uncle
or aunt or someone close to him had died. He just
broke down in tears and cried like a baby and
cared not at all that another person was there. How
uncomfortable Bennion had been with that display
of emotion, and yet he felt like doing the same
thing now, although he knew he wouldn't.

His thoughts were interrupted by a small boy
carrying a dish with some boiled beef and fried
bread. The child said nothing, only handed the
food to him and pointed to Helen Black Horse,
who looked over at him and tried to smile but man-
aged to nod her head to indicate that she had sent
the food for him. She didn't signal for him to come
over and he didn't, although for a long time after he
wished he had. A few minutes later he left.

The next day Black Horse was buried and
Bennion considered attending the funeral, but he
didn't. He thought of Doris Mae and decided to
stay away. He didn't know what she would do or
say if she saw him at the gravesite and he didn't
wish to risk an encounter that might prove to be
ugly or angry. He waited for the funeral and burial
to be over before he left Mission Town, already
having said his good-bys to the other Mormons on
the reservation, those few he cared anything about.

He drove west on Highway 83, but instead of turning north toward Murdo and Pierre, he drove on west until he came to the Parmelee Road and there he turned left and drove south toward Rosebud and the Ghost Hawk Park region.

The morning was cold, there was little wind, and the air felt like rain, still-needed rain. He drove toward the shadows of the Ghost Hawk Park but he would stop at the small cemetery on the hill before he reached the tall ponderosa pines that swept down into the park. His plan was simple. He would walk up to the grave, to that grassy knoll that looked so peaceful from the highway. He would stay a moment in the quietness of the spot, then get in his car and drive on home to Salt Lake Valley. He was certain now that this was to be the end of his church mission experience. He would not accept another assignment, no matter what was offered.

The car was warm, too warm, and he shut down the heater and opened the window and put out his arm and felt the drops of rain. The road was straight and flat and he could see the outline of the cemetery on the hill well before he got to it. At the turn-off that led out onto the prairie and a rough road up to the knoll he saw the coyote sitting watching him. The cunning creatures, he thought, had a way of knowing when there was danger and when there wasn't. Apparently this coyote knew Bennion wasn't someone to fear, for he didn't move for a long time. He just sat there grinning in the way coyotes like to do sometimes. Then the coyote ran, skirting the broken-down fence that surrounded the uneven crosses in the cemetery. Somehow, seeing that coyote made Bennion feel good and he almost laughed as he got out of the car and climbed the last few yards to the grave. He remembered how little he could get Black Horse to say about the coyote that had followed him on the snowy night the winter before, even though the incident provoked much talk all across the reservation. Everybody had his own theory about what it meant. Maybe even Black Horse saw the coyote as a sign that something bad was to happen, but if he did, he kept this to himself.

Bennion's father had told him that coyotes taught a man a lot about survival. He would have to remember to ask Pappy about this when he saw him next. Ask him what he thought seeing a lone coyote meant. Maybe he would have an explanation.